Tal —
the first of

Watch the Wall

A True Story of Smuggling & Injustice

Susan Ashcroft

Enjoy —

[signature]

OPOC

PUBLISHING

For David
whose wish it was to find an ancestor of note

Foreword

This novel is only twenty percent fiction. It would be reasonable to ask why I have not written a work of non-fiction – it would certainly have been easier. Had I done so I would be presenting the reader with a basket of facts with no apparent link between them.

Every incident here happened as written, though not always at the place and time given. Anyone interested enough to dissect it could be pointed towards the pile of source material which has been used as the basis of the work. Wherever possible quotations are given verbatim, indicated by the use of italics. I have taken dozens of disparate real-life incidents and placed them on a narrative arc that is entirely my own.

Watch the Wall is an attempt to bring to light something I have increasingly come to believe was a terrible, unforgivable wrong.

Susan Ashcroft, March, 2022

Five and twenty ponies,
Trotting through the dark -
'Brandy for the Parson,
Baccy for the Clerk.
Them that asks no questions
Isn't told a lie -
Watch the wall my darling
While the Gentlemen go by!

A Smuggler's Song
Rudyard Kipling

Preface

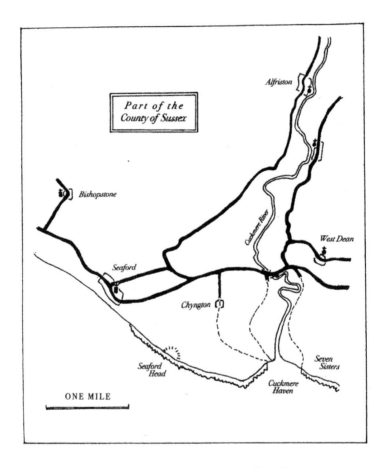

Map and original line drawings by Paul Jesson

Seaford, Sussex

April 8th, 1729, morning

See them there, Richard Ashcroft and his Jenny this bright spring morning. The blue of her dress matches the blue of her eyes and Richard thinks his heart will burst with the joy of it. In her hair, a garland. Flowers from the hedgerow intertwined with leaves from the big old oak on the common.

Watch them as they leave the church of St Leonard's in Seaford. There is a chill in the air, so they head straight to the Plough Inn just beside the lychgate.

Seaford Head rises on the horizon, basking in the sunshine, Cuckmere Haven nestling beneath it, the river winding all the way from there up to Alfriston and the Star Inn.

It's a small gathering. His parents, Richard and Sarah, hers, James and Mary, George Crawford, Richard's oldest friend, and his wife Dorothy.

The landlord and his wife are fond of Jenny. She has worked for them since she was twelve. Eight years gone in a flash and they have watched as Richard, after long days working in the fields, came regularly to slake his thirst and watch Jenny as she grew from child to beautiful young woman, now his wife.

'Look after my girl.' James looks fierce. He's not sure Richard has the means to give his daughter the life he wants for her but is happy for them anyway.

Hope spills out of them both, shining bright like her eyes; a cottage is already leased from Mr Palmer at Chyngton where Richard has laboured long and hard to build up enough money to ask Jenny to marry him.

Here they can raise their children securely and if it's on Mr Palmer's land Richard won't need to trudge miles back and forth every day, so will be able to watch them grow.

'Don't be silly Pa,' says Jenny. 'You just saw us promise to look after each other and we will!'

'Of course we will –' Richard hugs her to him 'in sickness and in health, richer and poorer, so long as we both shall live. I promise you James – I meant every word. Now buy me some beer!'

———

Houghton Hall, Norfolk
Afternoon, same day

See them there, First Lord of the Treasury Sir Robert Walpole and Thomas Pelham, Duke of Newcastle, walking the park at Houghton Hall on this fine spring afternoon. Newcastle's brother, Sir Henry Pelham, is a little way behind, deep in conversation with the Attorney General Sir Dudley Ryder. On the terrace Thomas Weaving is taking tea with the Widow Kesteven and William Castle but Sir Robert wishes they weren't. They are three of the biggest dealers in tea, coffee and spirits in London, here to interest him in their wares, but today is not the day.

'It's a fine house, Robert,' says the Duke, 'but will you see much of it when it's finished?'

Walpole stops at the edge of the ha-ha, gazes thoughtfully up the great walk towards Anmer in the distance, then turns back to admire the house, now so nearly finished. It has cost him dear and left him with mounting debts. He knows this means he cannot keep it purely for his own use and for the entertainment of his friends as he had originally intended – he must use it to make money.

An important decision has been made. 'I shall use it,' he says, 'to entertain great men. And while they're here I can let them know exactly what it is England wants of them. All great men have their price.'

See them there, the second set. Powerful pieces in the same puzzle – whose authority over the first set is total.

———

Seaford Head, Sussex
Night, same day

See them there, the five smugglers, waiting on a hillside near Seaford; looking far out to sea for a signal which is a long time coming.

George Crawford is with them. He had said goodnight to the wedding company an hour ago and made his way nonchalantly down Church Street, only starting to run when he reached the outskirts of town.

A flash, then another. 'Here we go,' mutters George, 'about bloody time!'

The five men begin the scramble down to the haven, cudgels in hand, moonlight glinting on pistols.

See them there, the third set. Final pieces in the jigsaw puzzle which, when completed, will reveal a picture so awful for Richard and his Jenny that it can scarcely be imagined.

Chapter 1

Chyngton, Sussex
Harvest 1729

'Something's not right with Jenny.' Richard and his mother sit in the shade of the oak taking their ease after a hard morning's harvesting. Families are dotted all over the field; food and drink have been sent down in a cart from the manor to keep them all refreshed – there can be no let up in their labours. The weather is fine and everyone must work till dusk to take advantage of it.

'It's hard in this heat, Richard.' He hardly needs to be told this. He has been scything since dawn while his mother and Jenny have followed, gathering the freshly cut corn into stooks to dry.

'I sent her off to the spring to get water. She'll be here in no time, ready to start again, and see, our strip is finished as well as any other. You worry too much – she's fine.'

'But that's just it. Last year she finished the whole morning without rest and then we sat here waiting for the cart to come from the manor.'

Any time alone with Jenny in a working day is precious to Richard which is why he loves harvest. For weeks he has looked forward to sitting with her here.

She still has not come. Sarah looks at her son fondly. His love for Jenny shows in his whole being and she thinks again how glad she is they found each other. She wonders if her own Richard, now in charge of the cart, ever worried about her in this way. Probably not, but they've been happy nevertheless.

'There she is!' He leaps to his feet and races towards her, hat in hand; she's lifted into the air, and he swings her round and round before leading her back to the tree. 'Sit, Jenny – I was worried about you – why did Mother need to send you for water?'

'It's hot Richard, I needed it and couldn't wait for Father and the cart. Mother knew she could easily finish the last little bit of the strip with you while I went to the spring. Really – it's nothing.'

Sarah has been watching their approach. She gets to her feet. 'I'll go with Father to take the cart back to the yard – you two stay here. There's a little while before we need to start on the next strip.' She turns back after a few yards. 'I'm glad you're well Jenny.'

The women nod gently to each other and on she goes. She turns again, but they have no thought for her now, together under the oak, so young, so hopeful. Sarah turns towards her husband, leaving the tree to the new generation.

Jenny sits with her back pressed against the trunk; her legs tucked up in front of her. She puts out her hand to her husband and pulls him gently down beside her. 'Why do you worry so, Rich? You've no reason.' She knows why but never tires of hearing it.

'You're just so precious to me Jen – I worry every day that I may somehow lose you and I couldn't bear it.'

Her bright mood darkens, but only a little. He is about to lose her in a way, and she knows she must tell him at last. Now would be perfect. She takes his face in her hands, kisses him gently as she turns him towards her. Looking into his eyes she wills him to guess her secret the way she's sure his mother has.

'You cannot have me to yourself forever, you know.' His worst fears flood to the front of his mind. 'Don't say so – why would you say so?' A simple man with a simple soul, he still has no idea, and she loves him too much to make him suffer.

'Richard, my love, I'm with child.'

Chapter 2

Bishopstone Place, Sussex
Home of the Duke of Newcastle

Thomas Pelham-Holles, 1st Duke of Newcastle, does not know it but he is always angry. Today he is at his Sussex home, Bishopstone Place, his favourite hunting seat, with plenty of reasons to be happy; it's August, he's here for the Lewes Races, has a houseful of agreeable guests and tonight most of the county will be coming to his lavish hunt ball. But underneath the urbane charm and the delight he showed this morning when he shot two hares (and again this afternoon when he shot the partridge), is the usual simmering anger.

Money. It always comes down to money.

His wife, who does not come here, thinks the furious, sullen aspect of his private face is down to excessive alcohol consumption, but she is wrong. These last few days he has remained sober, drunk nothing at all and done nothing but play whist with his guests at night.

No. It's the money. His opulent lifestyle, lived between his many estates (most in Sussex) and his London home at Newcastle House, must be kept up to a standard which leaves no apparent weakness for his political opponents to exploit.

Everything he has must be of the best quality. When he entertains, which he often does of course, it must be on the grandest scale. Not even his closest friends suspect what James Waller, his accountant and paymaster had told him yesterday.

Together they had viewed the preparations for the ball, and Mr Waller, after surveying the stock of claret, Burgundy, Champagne, Greek, Rhenish, Turkish, Hermitage, arrack and vintage port which was to provide the liquid refreshment at the ball (at a cost of eighteen guineas) had asked exactly how much the Duke was spending on this racing and hunting weekend.

'Something over £120, I imagine' had come the reply, which was what had led Waller to sit the Duke down in the library and stand over him as he went through the previous year's accounts.

INCOME
    Salary £6,589
    Trust £10,500
    Secret Service £711
    Prize in lottery £8
    Income from fines etc. £199
    Total £18,007

EXPENDITURE
    Housekeeping £4,000
    Private account £2,500
    Claremont, £3,800
    Sussex Estate and expenses £5,700
    Duchess £1,810
    TOTAL £17,810

. . .

Noting the profit of £197 for the year Newcastle had been jubilant, but this was short lived.

Reminding the Duke that to enable him to start paying off outstanding debts there had been an agreement to keep expenditure down to £12,000, Waller turned the page and revealed total debts which had had now risen to £21,846, no payments having been made against them in the past year.

Waller had been in no position to lecture the Duke or admonish him, but nevertheless Newcastle felt he had done both.

How is he supposed to manage on a £12,000 allowance? Something must change. If he is to spend more, he must increase his income and the only way he can do so is through his vast land holdings.

Walpole. He is the key to this. Newcastle must work out how to manipulate Walpole into freeing more money from his estates.

Then he might not need to be quite so angry.

Chapter 3

Cuckmere Haven, Sussex
Beneath the Seven Sisters

'There are men up there. I don't know what they're doing.'

Mark Moreton, leader of the gang, has been on guard, keeping watch while his men shuttle back and forth with the spirits which have just come in from France. George Crawford sets the barrel he has carried from the shore onto the pile growing nicely in the trees above Cuckmere Haven.

'Where? Who?' George follows Mark's gaze up to the top of the Seven Sisters, five hundred feet above.

'Could be customs men, but if they are, they're not patrolling. Go and see if they're any threat to us. No-one's come down here yet, but they will if they spot us.'

Not best pleased because the tide is high which means he must swim across to the cliff path, George does as he's told. Moreton is not a man to argue with.

He climbs warily. If there is a patrol it can come back at any time. As he goes, he keeps looking back down to see how things are going. The men ferrying goods can clearly be seen in the bright sunshine, but Moreton knows the revenue men do not expect smugglers to operate in broad daylight so only look for them at night, a dangerous thing to do from a cliff top.

Reflecting on this, George grudgingly acknowledges that Moreton is leader for good reason, but his own ambitions for leadership are becoming increasingly urgent. He will make a move soon.

At the top of the path, he finds a large white boulder roughly ten feet away from the cliff edge. He's walked this way many times before and not noticed it. Further on is another, also ten feet from danger, and beyond it yet one more. These are clearly markers, placed to catch moonlight and keep people away from the cliff's edge at night.

Only customs officers need to be able to walk this path in the dark as they make their way from the revenue building at Birling Gap to Cuckmere Haven in their pursuit of smugglers landing their cargos. It's a smart new initiative and Moreton did well to spot them.

George heads back down to the shore where the gang is resting together before heading off for the night, their work already done.

'They've marked a path to let them spy on us after dark.' George describes what he's seen. Moreton is thunderstruck. This is an unforeseen threat – up till now no-one has ventured along the cliff at night which has given him a valuable free hand.

'We need to get up there now.' It's George, not Moreton, who takes command. He has, after all, had time to think things through on his long trek back.

Moreton nods (he too needs time to think) and they all head across to the cliff path, mercifully no longer under water as the tide is now low.

'What's your plan?' Moreton knows George must have one, but there is no reply.

At the top it becomes clear.

'Move the stones lads – not too much, just a little for each one. Do it right and the devils will be no more threat to us.'

It's brilliant, of course. Moreton knows he would never have come up with it.

Under cover of darkness, with the stones now leading straight to death, the gang settles down to wait.

For his plan to work, George needs the customs patrol to be just one man – more will never fall for it. He reasons that the revenue will send out one officer who can quickly follow the stones back for help if he spots any activity below. He's right of course.

Twenty pairs of eyes, stationed safely in the dark behind the danger line, watch as the officer approaches, striding confidently as he follows his markers.

The scream as he goes over the edge rips chillingly through the night but does not stop. He has not fallen immediately to the beach below but hangs by his fingertips, scrabbling to get back up, calling on his mother for help, and pleading for mercy from he knows not who.

Moreton and George stand over him. The others wait.

It's clear that Moreton is not going to do it, so George does.

He stamps on the fingers, sending the man to his death and a message to any other revenue men trying to find a way to spy on them.

The men come forward, awestruck.

This is his moment; he lashes out and Moreton, too, is gone.

George turns and heads, deceptively nonchalant, back down the path to the shore, the men, now his, following him.

He's arrived.

Chapter 4

Chyngton, Sussex

Richard and Jenny's Cottage
1730

'He's beautiful.' Richard takes the mewling bundle from Goodwife Brewer and sees, for the first time, the face of his son.

'Jenny must rest, Richard. It was hard with her – I thought for a while she might die in the doing of it.'

'Die?' Richard recoils – finally acknowledging to himself that childbirth is no easy thing. He has spent much of the last thirty-six hours in the Plough, bolstered by tales from proud fathers who have been through all this many times before him. No-one mentions the women who have died. Their husbands are rarely seen in this company – they are too busy trying to bring up their children alone.

He and Jenny are happy in their cottage at Chyngton, just the two of them. But suddenly it seems small, smoky and dark. Their bed is above, a ladder giving access to it from the floor below. Till now this has served as living space for them, and it will shortly be the sleeping place for this new child and the others which may follow.

When he has been brave enough to come home, he has stood in the shadow of the cottage door, listening to the struggle playing out above; on none of those occasions did he stay very long – it was just too much to bear.

It's a mystery to him; what did the two women do up there? What has resulted in him being handed this beautiful bundle? What was happening to Jenny to make her scream so – to groan and pitifully call on him, her mother, her God, for help? What was the goodwife doing? Surely not just watching?

Goodwife Brewer has seen all this before. She long-since ceased to be amused by the ignorance of men and has given up hoping for change.

'Will she live?' Suddenly nothing matters so much. He pushes the baby back towards the goodwife, who, knowingly, refuses to take it. She understands that whatever the outcome here, Richard must take the child. If Jenny lives, they will both love and protect him fiercely. If she dies Richard will do so alone, she is sure. She's known him from the cradle – he's a good man.

But Jenny will live. She and Richard, each brought into the world by this same bent woman, will see the little man grow, thinks the goodwife, and work the land like their parents before them.

'She will recover, Richard, but I mean it when I say she needs rest. Take him. Have you named him?'

'James. James – for Jenny's father.'

'Of course.' She nods her approval as she climbs the ladder to fetch her few things. 'Jenny is sleeping, but you can come up now and wake her. Give her the child – he needs to suckle.'

After she has gone, Richard struggles to carry the precious gift up the ladder to his wife. Halfway up he stops and stares. Jenny is there, sleeping, beautiful. He, always amazed she is his, is again overwhelmed by the sight of her.

It's not just the relief, which is palpable; it is an indefinable

18

sense that she and this tiny new life are his. His to love and protect till his dying day.

'Jenny, love. Wake up.' He leans in and places James next to her on the mattress of straw. She stirs. Opens her eyes.

'Oh Richard – is it over?'

'Aye. We have a boy. Here he is – our James.'

She looks into the eyes of her son for the first time and wraps him in her love like every mother before her. She quietly sets about giving him the nourishment he eagerly seeks.

How does she know how to do this?

Richard can only watch and wonder.

Chapter 5

Seaford, Sussex

Church of St Leonard

'Dost thou, in the name of this child, renounce the devil and all his works, the vain pomp and glory of the world, with all covetous desires of the same, and the carnal desires of the flesh, so thou wilt not follow nor be led by them?'

The Reverend John Ballard has been in his Seaford parish for twenty years. He knows his flock. He also knows full well that at least one of these godparents cannot answer the question truthfully if the christening is to continue.

Jenny clasps James to her and looks expectantly at George who is hesitating.

It should not be difficult for a man like him to lie – his whole way of life is a lie – but to do it in the house of God is hard. He sees Jenny waiting.

'She has the most beautiful eyes,' he thinks, 'always full of hope. Is it possible she has no idea what I do?'

Richard is watching George. He knows his friend is trapped and finds it amusing.

No way out for George.

'I renounce them all' he says, exactly as his sister and his wife did, just before him.

The minister takes these renunciations at face value, not for the first time. It's a simple thing for him. God already knows it all anyway, and the minister has a child to save.

'James. I baptise thee in the name of the Father, and of the Son, and of the Holy Ghost.'

The water in the font is shockingly cold and the baby squirms in the old man's arms. He's relieved to hand James back to his mother. The years are passing and one of these days he's going to drop one of these bundles, but not this time.

Turning to George, Jane and Dorothy he continues: 'You must remember; it is your duty to see James be taught, so soon as he shall be able to learn, what a solemn vow, promise and profession hath here been made by you this day. And it is your solemn duty to see this child virtuously brought up to lead a godly and a Christian life.'

'Richard and Jenny can do that,' thinks George. 'For my part, I shall see him kept safe as far as I can, and well provided for, as much as Richard will let me.'

They leave the church, happy to have it all over. Jenny and Dorothy have brought a picnic for them all to share under the oak tree. Richard proudly nurses his newly baptised son while the women fuss over food.

George has somewhere else to be.

'Richard come with me?' He is aware of the increasing divide between himself and his friend. As far as he can tell, the arrival of James has made Richard and Jenny happier than ever. They are content for Richard to stay as he is, eking out an adequate but unexciting living from his strips of land with no ambition to do anything else.

George is cut from different cloth. Money is coming to him

in ever-increasing amounts these days and his love for his friends makes him want to share it.

'Stop now George. It's not for me. Go and do what you must do. I'm happy here beneath this tree with Jenny and James. I'm content. Leave me. I will not do anything which would risk leaving them alone.'

'Does Jenny know how much you could be bringing her – where she could live, what she could own?'

'Of course. No-one hereabouts doesn't know what you do George, and we wish you well. But your life is not for all of us. Ours is settled. And here.'

Chapter 6

Seaford, Sussex
The Road to West Dean
1732

George sees much less of Richard and Jenny now that James, two, and the new baby are taking up so much of their time. He was welcomed with open arms today, delighted with his godson who smiled and cooed in response to his clumsy efforts to entertain him; he even tried to hold the new baby Mary Lucy for a while, but handed him back to Jenny as soon as he could.

Richard is content with home and family; part of George envies him that strength and wishes that he could be so easily satisfied, but he's not such a man.

He knows his way of life is dangerous and usually short lived, but it brings with it rewards too great for him to resist. Richard will make old bones. He will not.

Preoccupied, he turns his horse Dandy towards West Dean. It's September already and one day soon he will have storage and tunnels under his new Lewes house, but he does not have such luxuries now. His immediate problem is what to do with the hundred and forty-four sheepskins he needs to take to France.

He watched the sheep sales on the green at Jevington and

took note of those which would end up within two miles of John Allen's shop in West Dean.

His most trusted men have spent the last few days buying their skins. A few here and there quickly added up to the gross he was looking for, and all are now safely stored behind Allen's shop.

The stash cannot stay secret long, so he must move them quickly. First, they must be packed up – twelve to a pack – and then they must be got down to the boats waiting to take him to France to sell them.

He and his companions will lead a train of packhorses down from West Dean, roughly following the winding Cuckmere to the haven under cover of darkness tomorrow night.

He may not have had much in the way of schooling, but he knows his men gave 1/- a skin and they were paid £2 a man for their efforts. £10 in total for his men, £7 for the skins and £20 for the boatmen to take him over the channel. He can't reckon his total costs – but he knows they're a long way short of the £150 he will get for the skins in France.

The fancy London tradesmen call this profit. They buy from him because his goods cost much less than those from legitimate, highly taxed sources. They are respected men; respected for their substance – their shop fronts and fine houses. He knows they supply tea, coffee and alcohol to people in high places who, in return for cheap goods, ask no questions about the means of supply.

George's sales continue at pace. His warehouse in Stockwell is left unharried. He does not wish to think about this too closely and has no idea how long the unspoken arrangement can last.

He has watched and learned. He knows the profit he makes on selling wool abroad will buy him brandy and tea to sell in

London. And if his customers can also make profit, he will be left largely alone. And so, the world turns.

Chapter 7

Seaford, Sussex

The Plough Inn
1734

Richard has arrived in the Plough exhausted after a long day's labour in the fields. James, Mary Lucy and newly arrived Dickon let him have very little sleep these days and Jenny, though a good cook, has little to forage at this time of year. It's quite possible the beer, bread and cheese George has just bought for him will provide most of his nourishment today.

The friends have much less in common these days. Richard thinks of little but Jenny and the children, while George is consumed by the running of his gangs and ever-increasing trade. He needs help from someone he can trust, knows that nothing could make Richard betray him, but even now cannot find any way to persuade him to join him.

'You're a fool.' George looks at his friend steadily, willing him to see that his life does not have to be the way it is. 'You and Jenny can have whatever you want. The money's not hard to come by. What's stopping you? Don't she and the children deserve better?'

Richard shakes his head vigorously. 'Of course they do. They deserve better'n me that's for sure, but Jenny chose me, and I want everything they have to come from me – honestly earned. Besides, to do what you do, I would need things about me I just don't have. Devilment, courage – even cruelty if you're in a tight squeeze. And you need your wits about you all the time. I couldn't do it; you know I couldn't.'

George gives a half smile. In truth, he knows Richard wouldn't be the best smuggler in the world. Too soft, too trusting, too besotted with his wife and children, too homespun to be a brigand and too honest to be able to make convincing pretence of being one.

'Won't you at least come and see my new house?' George is immensely proud of his town house in Lewes, just over an hour's ride away. He knows its handsome frontage marks him out as someone with money, if not power.

He also knows its elevated position gives plenty of room for storage underneath it and will allow him to tunnel right onto the marshes by the Ouse. From there he can transport goods north to his customers in London or south to the channel at Newhaven for boats to France and beyond.

'Why do you want a new house – and why not here in Seaford? This is home. Your friends and family are all here.'

George is silent. Can Richard really be so naive? Forget the tunnels. Think of the prestige. Houses like his on School Hill can't be found in Seaford, and he means to use it to step up in life, taking his family, if not his friend, with him.

'Dorothy will live better there. We shall be comfortable at last – and think of the schooling.'

'But you're away from home all the time – how is that comfortable?' Richard couldn't leave Jenny and the children; probably not even for one night; it's the main reason he cannot contemplate joining George in whatever scheme he is inviting him into.

Why he cannot get his friend to see they are happy as they

are, he has no idea. He wants better for him, he knows. But Richard thinks they have enough. They have a home, he has a plentiful supply of work, he can get firewood, berries and game from common land; they are never cold or really hungry. It's enough.

'Would you not want Jenny to be comfortable and have good things? Beautiful gowns? Jewels?'

Richard is genuinely puzzled by this suggestion. Where would they go with such things? Supper every so often with Mr Palmer in his kitchen is the most they ever venture out for, and gowns and jewels are not needed for such evenings.

'We don't need those here,' he looks round the bar and laughs at the very idea.

'Surely you want good schooling and friends for your children?'

'We've both done well without schooling, and what better friend do I need than you? James and the others will find good friends of their own here in the village – just as I did.'

It's George's turn to shake his head now. 'I hope it's always so, Rich. Surely a little something stashed away against harder times wouldn't be so very bad even if you won't move? Will you at least come and see the house – there is work to do there which would pay well. I will need strong men about me for what I'm planning.'

Richard drains his tankard and slams it down. He wishes George were not so persistent.

'Enough man. We are happy. I can earn what we need – have done for five years now. It's our way of life – same as my father's before me and his before that. It's a good life. I've no wish or need to change it. Besides, our old nag would never make it to Lewes!'

George gives up. His tankard joins Richard's on the bar. 'I have to go.'

Richard addresses his friend's departing back; 'Be careful George. You're a good friend to me. Please take care.'

George is gone. Richard has no idea where the meet is tonight and doesn't want to know. A wave to the publican and he is out of there too. Off home to Jenny.

He feels good.

Chapter 8

Chyngton, Sussex

Richard and Jenny's Cottage

When he gets home, Richard finds Jenny has spent the evening with George's wife. Dorothy Crawford is older than her, but they have been friends since George brought her to the village as his new wife ten or more years ago.

Jenny and Dorothy had shared a meagre meal from the pot over the fire and, as always of late, Jenny had tried to make sense of the life Dodo now leads with George.

She knows he's a smuggler, and she supposes Dodo knew it before they got married. But Jenny doesn't think she could have known George's rapidly changing fortunes would propel her out of the village to live amongst the fashionable folk in Lewes, which is what they had talked about all evening.

'The house is enormous Jen. I'm not fit to run such a place. What will we do with all those rooms?' Jenny had tried to imagine herself with such a problem. She couldn't see it and had no answer.

'George is away so much of the time these days – how am I to be mistress of such a house? I have no idea where to start and I'm quite sure the neighbours won't be offering much help.

Please Jen – can't you persuade Richard to come and work with George so we can all live together? I know it's George's dearest wish – he doesn't want to leave you two behind here when we go. Come with us – please.'

Jenny reassures her husband that she had explained yet again how grateful they were, but there was nothing about the potential grand new life in Lewes they would want for themselves. Besides, both she and her husband have grave doubts about George's way of life and know Richard is not cut out for it.

If Richard took to smuggling, Jenny knows her own life would be one of permanent, crippling worry. Dodo doesn't seem to suffer this – perhaps because George's mysterious absences are nothing new, just steadily increasing in number, and becoming an unspoken, indefinable danger which can only get worse. She fears for her friend.

'Can't you get him to stop, Dodo? He could use the money from the Lewes house for you to live comfortably round here for years. You could buy the Plough. Surely it must be worth thinking about?' Jenny is braver than her husband. He never ventures onto this ground.

Dorothy had smiled at the suggestion and then looked slowly round the shabby little cottage in which they were sitting. George had picked her for a reason. However hard it would be for her to turn herself into a reasonably passable lady she would do it in the end. She had steel in her, as had he, and both were trapped by beckoning riches. Too late for either of them to change.

'What if you get sent to the colonies?' Jenny could think of no fate worse but had no real idea what, or where, the colonies were. She did know that criminals were sent there regularly.

'George is clever. I have his promise – he will stop long

34

before it comes to that, and I believe him. Besides, I can think of far worse things that could happen.'

Both women had sat silent for a while, a chill running down at least one spine.

All this is told to Richard on his return. He thinks it strange how he and George have wives who suit each of them so well, and lucky too. How awful it would be if he and Jenny did not agree that their life here was perfect for them.

'Are you happy here with me Jen?' He thinks he'd better check, just in case.

'No need to ask, my love. You know I am'.

Chapter 9

Chyngton, Sussex

Richard and Jenny's Cottage
1735

'He's coming, he's coming!' James, now five, has been watching at the door for his father to come home. Jenny hears him but cannot stop him. He's off down the lane, throwing himself at Richard, hanging onto his legs for dear life, sobbing and choking – trying to get him to understand how hard it has been, the wait.

'What's amiss Jamie?' Richard untangles him and hoists him up to try and make sense of this. It's past midnight. Jamie should have been asleep for hours. Richard has been waiting to meet George in the Plough, but for some reason he did not appear tonight and Richard has finally headed home.

'Oh hurry – it's Mary Lucy – she's sick. Mother has been trying and trying to help her but nothing's working. Ma's crying. Dickon and Ann are crying. You must come and make everything right again.'

Mary Lucy? His beautiful daughter had been fine this morning. Three years old and the prettiest little maid you could imagine. She had 'helped' him with his boots and had stood in the door until he was out of sight, her little brother Dickon peeping out from behind her. Just like any other working day.

'Come on Jamie, show me.' He puts the boy down and starts to run, leaving the child to follow as best he can.

'Richard? Where have you been? Help me – please help me. It's Mary Lucy.' The anguish in the voice from the loft chills him to the bone.

To Jamie: 'Look after Dickon and Ann.' He has seen the little ones cowering in the corner downstairs, alone for he knows not how long. The ladder to the loft is still hard for them to climb, so the boys would never have followed their mother up there even if they hadn't been too afraid to try. He lifts Ann from the floor and onto the bed, gesturing to Jamie to join her there with Dickon and wait.

James and Mary Lucy share the loft. Dickon and Ann still stay with their mother and father downstairs in the big room where they all live and eat. Richard's up the ladder now, chest and head above the floor. Jenny is clutching Mary Lucy, her face glistening in the candlelight, wet with tears. There is no room for him while Jenny is there.

'Leave her, Jen and come down. Let me up to see what can be done.' Jenny's reaction is violent. She hugs the child to her even tighter. For the first time, Richard realises Mary Lucy is not making any sound.

'Jen, come, please. Let me see. What is it?'

'She took sick this morning and I sent her up here to sleep. But she couldn't sleep, she was so sick. I purged her, God help me, I shook her – I tried everything to stop it, but nothing worked. I daredn't leave her except to fetch water to try and see would she drink, but she took nothing. Then there was fever – she was red hot. I climbed up to watch her and hold her – she was so frightened – I couldn't leave her.'

'Did you go up to the house, to Mrs Palmer? To the village, to the goodwife?'

'Are you listening to me, Rich? I couldn't leave her, I just couldn't. Jamie tried to go up to the house, but he was too frightened and said he couldn't find the way. I don't know how far he went. Not far enough, anyway.'

In his heart he knows. He knows but does not want to know. He curses himself for not coming straight home after finishing today's hedging, for waiting so long for George, not sure whether this might have made any difference at all.

He hears himself, not so long ago: 'It's a good life. I've no wish or need to change it.'

What a fool he was not to know change comes whether we will it or not.

And it has surely come to them now.

Chapter 10

Houghton Hall, Norfolk
The Dining Room
1736

'The King!' Walpole raises his glass. 'The King!' comes the reply. The ladies signal to each other and leave the room. The Duke of Newcastle, his wife safely out of the way, relaxes.

He catches Walpole's eye over his raised glass and holds it steadily.

'So, Robert – why have you really invited me to Houghton today?'

'Why would I not? We are good friends. The hunting was excellent.'

Walpole has held Newcastle's gaze but he is the first to drop his eyes.

Newcastle stands, walks to the wall and opens the concealed door in the panelling to reveal a very small privy. Without closing the door behind him, he takes time to relieve himself before returning to his seat. He hates having to wait for the ladies to leave before he can do this, but he is a man who knows how to be careful of his manners when it matters.

'Indeed, it was – but you're a very busy man. Too busy for

hunting parties without purpose. What is it you want me to do for you?' Newcastle is nothing if not direct.

A smile of acknowledgement. 'You know me well, Thomas.' A shrug, and out it comes.

'I need your support to stop the King declaring war on Spain. He is impatient. Repeated attacks and plundering of our ships by the Spaniards cannot be tolerated but I must have time to try and get them stopped through diplomatic means. The country cannot afford war and I do not think the populace is hungering after it in any way. Such a conflict would be pointless and must be avoided at all costs. With your help I can stop the King pursuing this foolishness, but even if he insists on fighting he must have the assent of Parliament. If we work together I believe we will narrowly have enough support to stop any order getting through. Once I tell him I have the numbers to defeat any proposal of war he will back down.' A pause. 'Your support won't go without advantage to yourself.' This last is an apparent afterthought, but both men know it's the crux of the matter.

Newcastle savours the wine. He has problems of his own which have nothing to do with Spain. He urgently needs money, and he must also deal with the threat of French troops landing in Sussex.

Thousands of troops are rumoured to be gathering at Dunkirk, Calais and Boulogne getting ready to attack the south coast of England, land an army in support of the Young Pretender, and unseat the King. Born and raised in Germany, George II has never been popular and is still seen as foreign.

The last thing Newcastle wants is for any of his lands to be turned into a battlefield. There is real danger of this, but he does not judge it to be imminent. The money problem comes first.

Walpole needs help to stop a Spanish war immediately or

the country will be bankrupt. Newcastle knows he can extract a price for lending his help, which is an opportunity not to be missed. He can solve his money problems here, today. The French threat can wait a while yet.

'You're asking me to take great personal risk – the King is not a forgiving man. He is hell-bent on the idea of punishing the Spanish. Why on earth should I do this?' he empties his glass, leans back and waits.

'What can I give you in return for your support, Thomas? What do I have that you want?'

The answer has been long-prepared. Newcastle has always known Walpole could be made to buy his support someday.

What he wants is the freedom to exploit his enormous landholding to the full; he is currently stopped from doing this by traditional strip-farming practices.

'Sussex, Robert, give me Sussex.'

'Sussex? You and Richmond own it already between you – it's hardly any sort of reward!'

Newcastle is suddenly angry again. Is Walpole being deliberately obtuse?

'I am not asking you to give me what I already own. If you want me to risk my reputation before Parliament and the King you must give me Sussex in the truest sense. Yes, Richmond and I own it between us – but we don't control it.'

So that's it. Walpole sees what Newcastle is asking in return for support to stop a Spanish war and knows it will cost him nothing.

'Enclosure? You want smooth passage for the enclosure of your lands?'

'We have all seen the benefits enclosure has brought in Northumberland. Taking control of the common lands, doing away with the inefficiency of the strips – it allows landowners to put money in their purses. A great deal of money. They can raise the rents of the bigger farms to levels they could only dream of before. Modern farming methods bring efficiencies, increased crops and much less trouble from the peasants – they will be gone at last.

'I've asked you to support this for years, but you have always pushed me back, saying I must wait for the tenants to come to their own arrangements about the strips; until they come up with their own voluntary plan for larger, more efficient farms, I must wait. I know the Duke of Richmond has been waiting for at least two years while they have been arguing in Goodwood, trying to beat out a plan to redistribute the strips. Chichester is the same – and I see it in Seaford and Eastbourne – all my Sussex lands.

'It will never be settled. It's not in the tenants' interests to come to agreement. A small number of them will benefit from the ability to farm the larger farms for us – at a decent rent, yes. But most of the men who have been working my land for centuries will no longer have a place there. Their rights to common land – to grazing the animals, gathering firewood, foraging for food – will all be gone. It's no small thing we are asking them to decide and no, it really isn't in their best interests to agree to it, but it is in ours.' By which, he means his.

Walpole waits, apparently hesitating, but this is just for show. He will let Newcastle finish putting his case before giving him what he wants.

'We all saw what happened in Northumberland. The benefits of the larger, enclosed farms are beyond question. Modern methods raise yields beyond our wildest dreams. And as for the poorer tenant farmers, they can all move to the towns and find work there. It will be a short sharp pain, but things will come right for them soon enough.'

Walpole looks doubtful at this. 'Really?'

'Altruism is not something I've often seen displayed by you,

Robert.' Newcastle knows he's almost there. Surely Walpole won't deny him this?

Time for double bluff.

'You told me to let them decide. Better coming from them, you said, less trouble. I should wait, you said. Perhaps you were right.' He shrugs. The unspoken message is clear; block me on this and there will be war with Spain.

Walpole has finished pretending. It's a much easier deal than he had been expecting.

'Well, if there is an Act of Enclosure they won't have to decide. You can do it for them. You've waited long enough. If you give me your support and persuade Richmond to join you in voting down the war, if necessary, in committee, I will see Sussex is enclosed by a simple Parliamentary Act in the next session. Six good men is all it needs for the commission – we would be three – three more will not be hard to find.'

'Richmond will be delighted. I don't think I will have any trouble persuading him that war in Spain is not in any of our interests.' Nor, he thinks, will Richmond miss the point. Voting the war down will be entirely in interests of his own. Goodwood will be free at last.

'And you guarantee the enclosure of Sussex in return?' One last check.

'I do.' Walpole raises his glass. 'Another toast Thomas; enclosure!'

Hundreds of good men and their families homeless, just like that.

Newcastle isn't quite so angry now.

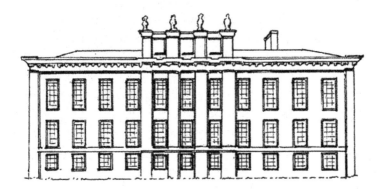

Chapter II

Kensington Palace, London
The Throne Room

'Sir Robert. I hope you are well.' The greeting is formal, and that of a man not speaking his native tongue. Though German born, King George's first language is French, but business must be carried out in English here in London.

The hairs on the back of his neck immediately tell Walpole all is not well. The King does not turn to face his old friend but continues staring into the courtyard below. Frederick Louis, Prince of Wales, struts triumphantly across it; he knows he has landed a fatal blow.

'You asked for an audience Robert. What is it?'

'Sire, two things.'

The King keeps watching the yard. He already knows what's coming, but the scene must play out.

'The first?'

'The first is to plead with you to think again about starting a war with Spain. I think I have the numbers in Parliament to stop you doing so. The cost would be ruinous to the country, and I do not believe the people will feel strongly enough about a few plundered ships to maintain support for ruinous conflict.

Silence.

'Newcastle and Richmond are with me, and this will give us the majority.' He presses on with his request, but the threat is not being received in the way he expected.

'Newcastle?' The King turns at last to face him. 'What was his price?'

'Enclosure, your majesty, particularly in Sussex. It requires your consent.'

The King looks suddenly old, well beyond his fifty-nine years. He thinks for a while, then speaks.

'As for the idea of war, I am already weary of it. Holding back for the time being is not the great concession it would have been several months ago.' He pauses before delivering the next news.

'Newcastle has already been granted his wish for enclosure, Robert. I gave the order for the Act this morning. There, I am afraid, our conversation must end.'

Walpole takes an involuntary step backwards. The King gave the order this morning? Before he could raise the matter himself? Something is seriously wrong.

'Majesty?'

'I have again quarrelled with Freddy about Spain, Robert. Newcastle was with him. They told me this morning that Parliament will not agree to it and I have agreed not to pursue it at this time.'

So. Walpole now sees that, rather than helping him stop George from starting a war with Spain, the Duke has forced the issue himself and claimed all the credit for saving the King's face. In return, he has been given the enclosure of Sussex, exactly what Walpole himself had promised him.

The balance of power between the King and The Prince of Wales has changed and Newcastle – Newcastle! – has taken advantage and made it all happen already. How? Why has he not been warned? His networks have broken down. There are new powers rising in the land.

His only thought echoes the King's; what was Newcastle's price? Surely not just enclosure, which he was getting anyway.

The King turns back to the window and watches as Newcastle climbs into Prince Frederick's carriage. After what feels to Walpole like an eternity the King turns wearily back to him.

'Newcastle tells me the numbers in both houses are now very finely balanced Robert. He has made it clear that I cannot be sure of his support in future. He will work with the Prince of Wales.'

The King, Newcastle and Walpole have been working together for a very long time and this betrayal is a hammer blow. A rueful smile crosses his face; no point fighting. It has been too well organised.

'I'm struck dumb, Majesty.'

The King has the good grace to look discomforted but says nothing.

'Things are conspiring against us Robert. There will eventually be war with Spain and it will have to be funded. Parliament must be led by those who can assist me and their leader is now Newcastle. It will suit him for you to remain as Prime Minister until he knows you can no longer be of use to him. When that time comes he will turn the house against you and force you to step down.

'Newcastle is the most ambitious man I know, here or anywhere else. He is also clever. He craves power but does not want to be seen wielding it. I am quite sure that in the end he will persuade my son to help him put his brother into your office.

'When the time comes, I will be given no choice. Henry

Pelham will be Prime Minister – a man too weak to do anything but answer to his brother.'

As he leaves the palace for the lonely journey back to Norfolk, Walpole knows he has made the most basic mistake – he has allowed himself to forget that no politician should ever give anyone absolute trust. For the remainder of his time in office, Walpole will dance to the tune of Newcastle, the man he trusted – and others will pay the price.

Chapter 12

Chyngton, Sussex
The Village Green
1737

Richard sits with his back to his favourite tree. He has done this since he was first able to leave the farm on his own. He didn't know then, and can barely articulate now, that this oak has stood here for many years, maybe hundreds. It has weathered storms – even a tornado – and watched his ancestors as their lives unfolded. Births, childhoods, loves, marriages, feuds, illnesses, deaths, happiness, misery. He has passed this tree every day of his life, not sparing it much thought, but invisibly sustained by it. Always there. Always was, always will be, just as he, his grandparents, his mother and father, and now his own family, Jenny, James, Dickon and Ann have been.

Except. Now he knows it might not always be there. He is sitting with his back pushed against the familiar trunk as if being able to feel it hard enough through his jerkin will somehow make everything come right. Surely the tree will stand, and he and Jenny will bring their grandchildren to sit underneath its canopy in their final years?

But they won't. He knows they won't because Mr Palmer told him so this morning. Somehow, he must tell Jenny they have to leave the land they grew up on, have worked on, their parents and grandparents have lived on. He must tell her it is no longer available to them. They must leave. Not today but very soon.

Palmer, his landlord, must leave too. All part of the enclosure of Lord Newcastle's lands which begins next month. The strips will be hedged and fenced off into big, efficient, productive private fields. Worse, the common will also be enclosed so Richard and all the other Richards have nowhere to graze their cows and sheep. Nowhere for their chickens to run. No milk, no meat, no eggs. Nowhere to forage – no berries, no nuts, no sorrel. No firewood.

No firewood. Firewood is no use if you have no hearth to bring it to, and Richard already knows they will have neither hearth nor home here for much longer. No-one will. He cannot think where they are to go and fears they will have to throw themselves onto the mercy of the parish.

Mr Palmer has a choice of sorts. Newcastle has offered him his home at a rent raised beyond all imagining. He can pay for it – or try to – with the money he will be paid to work the new farm for his master, no longer in command of his own fate. But he can, at least, accept it and survive.

Richard has no such choice. Palmer will have no work to give him and no tiny cottage to rent to him in return. The cottage is in the middle of what will be the new estate and will be gone, along with all the others, before the year is out.

Richard learned all this today. Palmer was sorry, really sorry, but now has problems of his own. He knows, of course he knows, that Richard and Jenny, already impoverished and still grieving Mary Lucy, are facing destitution. He is powerless to stop it but pragmatic enough to pass on the news and move on.

It starts next month. The tree will go, taking their history and all their hopes with it.

Chapter 13

Bishopstone, Sussex
Bridge over the Creek

Richard, Jenny and George stand on the old bridge, looking out over the creek near Bishopstone towards the sea.

Richard still cannot fathom what has happened to him and his precious family. Much of what he knew is gone. He still has Jenny and his three remaining children, but the strips of common land, farmed by Ashcrofts for generations, have been taken by Act of Parliament and absorbed into the farmland of the Duke of Newcastle so quickly they hardly had time to realise what was happening.

They have fared better than many. Mr Palmer has interceded with Newcastle on Richard's behalf, and he has been given work fishing in the creek and helping with the heavy labour of digging out the tidal reservoir for a proposed new tide mill.

However, Newcastle's generosity in providing work did not extend to finding shelter for them. For the months before they came here they stayed in George's Lewes town house where Jenny acted as maid and Richard as labourer in the cellars and tunnels George is having constructed underneath it. Even this felt too risky an enterprise for Richard, so the extraordinary news that George has brought them a small place to live above the creek where he will be working has brought joy to them all.

'We can never thank you enough for our new home George.' Jenny could weep with relief and looks at her husband's best friend with new eyes. She knows who he is and what he does and has always been afraid his constant entreaties for Richard to join him in smuggling would persuade her gentle husband to give in in the end.

But Richard has been steadfast. Farming is all he knows but, if he can no longer do it, he is determined this new life in Bishopstone is the way he can look after her and their family without breaking the law.

'It's little enough. I hate to see you having to live so.' George turns and looks towards what is barely more than a hovel, a run down wooden cabin halfway between the coast and the village. It is, in his eyes, a mean place, barely habitable but at least dry, with enough room for them all at a pinch but, most importantly, near the creek where the reservoir is to be built so Richard can be close to some work and be able to feed them.

George has continued to offer his friend well-paid work with the smuggling teams carrying goods across the channel or up to London. Richard could do any number of things working for his friend here in Bishopstone but is adamant he won't do any of them. It would bring him security of a sort, but breaking the law is not for him. To live in constant conflict and fear of discovery would destroy him.

It has been hard enough to accept the cabin, so generously given. He has only been able to take it as payment in return for his underground labours in Lewes, but they all know this is far more than he has earned. A permanent home with no rent for the rest of their lives is more than they could have dreamed of.

It's a small thing to George – probably less than the cost of a single night's work for him, but to them it's the world. The Bishopstone cabin is now their home and even Parliament cannot take it from them.

Richard has been studying the creek and ponds from the bridge, looking beyond the area he will be helping to dam for the reservoir. 'I can fish for the Duke from here, and there are oyster beds down there too. We won't starve.'

'You can give me fish to take home for tea when I'm on watch then.' George comes this way regularly as his goods come in and out from France. It's a remote and mysterious place and he has come to know it well. He knows he can outwit any customs man who comes looking for him here. In truth, he knows that having Richard on hand might be useful, though he would never say so.

'Tell me again, George; why are we making a reservoir?' Richard is happy to do it, but the plan makes no sense to him.

'To hold the water as it flows under the bridge here at high tide. In time there will be a mill on this bridge and the water will turn the wheels as it flows in and out again with the tides. More money for Newcastle – he has the land to grow the wheat now and here in the new mill he will have somewhere to turn it into flour.'

Richard looks around him. It is an incomprehensible plan to him. The bridge has always been here – a mill on top of it? He shrugs. If people want to pay him to get this nonsense started, he will happily take their money.

But he is much more excited about the fish.

Chapter 14

Cuckmere Haven, Sussex

The Seashore
1738

George waits just before dawn, ready to go up-river to the traditional staging post at the Market Cross House in Alfriston with his newly imported tea and brandy. The cellars at Market Cross must do the job for a while longer – his own new house in Lewes is not yet adapted to his purpose.

George's house will not match the twenty-one rooms, six staircases, forty-eight doorways and maze of passageways at Market Cross (all of which have made for easy escape from confused customs men for at least a hundred years) but it will have many more cellars and a labyrinth of escape tunnels underneath it. Best of all it will be hiding in plain sight in the middle of the town. No-one has been bold enough to make such a place the centre of a wide-spread smuggling organisation before. George is very pleased with himself for coming up with this.

Because he has been well known throughout the area since childhood it is his real name he uses here. He has learned how to dress, how to speak and how to blend into these new surroundings and in the even fancier places of trade belonging to his London customers. No-one in Lewes or London will ever suspect he is the leader of the most ruthless network of gangs across Sussex.

He has been back from France a week now. He had a good time spending the money from the sale of his fleeces. Fine food and wine are becoming more familiar to him and soon he will have them at home every day. Wryly he tells himself there's no going back from this way of life – too much to lose – but he is pretty sure it will end badly.

The trip hadn't been easy. The English Channel is very busy these days. The navy is on permanent patrol – even in the small Rye boat he was travelling in it had been hard not to be seen.

Once in France he realised they had, perhaps, been seen, but they were of no interest to the navy ships which were watching out for French troops crossing the channel en masse to unseat the King.

George has a hazy understanding of this but, having established first-hand that small boats can still cross navy lines unharmed, he cannot see it is any threat to him. It's the customs patrols he needs to worry about.

A single light comes bobbing onto the horizon. There should be more than one. Is this another boat on his patch, invading his turf? He pulls out his pistol and waits before heading down to the shore.

Agonisingly slowly the craft comes fully into view, and he recognises it as one of his own. A boat coming home alone can only mean one thing. Something has gone disastrously wrong. Where are the other five?

He wades out to help drag the vessel in, barely able to contain himself till all are safely on land.

'What happened?' His men are bedraggled and very frightened. George's rages are fierce and cruel.

'The revenue men came at us out of the mist. We had to jump for freedom. Lucky we were close to shore, or we would all be drowned.'

The fury rises in him. The Rye boats had been to pick up thirty casks of brandy and two tons of tea – his return for all his effort with the latest batch of sheep. Somehow word has got out and the plan has gone badly wrong.

'Where's the cargo?' he yells 'Who has it? Tell me now or I'll cut out your tongues, all of you.' If they notice he doesn't ask about his missing men, they don't say so.

'They took it to the customs house. I think it's still there, but so is the navy with guns trained on the doors.' Jeremiah Hardy, now George's second in command, is bolder than the rest but stays within the crowd for safety.

'We'll see about that,' George is heading for his horse. 'Meet me here at sundown with horses and weapons. We'll take it back. Tonight.'

'Be sensible man, let it go. It's just the one cargo. We can't take on the navy!'

But this is George Crawford; known to his men now as Black Diamond. 'Sundown,' he says, 'tonight.'

He mounts Dandy and wheels up onto the cliff path, spurring the horse on as he tries to gallop off his anger, heading instinctively towards the customs house.

Calming somewhat, he slows to a trot. He needs to think clearly if this is to be put right. None too soon he comes to his senses and realises galloping straight into the sight of the navy is not what he should be doing.

Warily he goes the last mile on foot, leaving the horse tethered in a copse behind him. The customs house stands behind the small ridge above him, its doors covered by the guns on the naval vessel, exactly as he has been told.

Defeated, he drops down onto the bank and stands

watching half-heartedly for the next hour. He detects no movement from anyone other than the gunners, so concludes the rest of the crew is in town celebrating the capture of his cargo. He briefly considers heading into town to pick a fight but knows it would serve no useful purpose. He stands glaring at the ship, thinking he should just go home.

He sits down in despair, looks at the customs house and realises that from this lower point of view he can see less of it because it is now half covered by the ridge. He throws himself onto his back. Laid flat he cannot see it at all. He looks from ship to ridge and back again. And again; and begins to calculate.

Chapter 15

Beyond Birling Gap, Sussex
The Customs House

They edge towards the customs house, dark lanterns turned away from the coast. The horses, thirty of them, are being held a few hundred yards back by ten of his men who are waiting for his signal to come forward.

The other twenty are crawling, blindly following their leader below the ridge line, waiting for the gunfire they are sure will start at any moment. They get to the doors. Still nothing happens.

George is now certain his calculations are correct. The tide has gone out. The navy ship has dropped, and the building can no longer be seen from its deck. He is gambling that the men on board will not realise this. The officers have left the ship; the seamen who remain are not expecting trouble and assume they have enough firepower to deal with anything that comes up. They do not know, or do not care, that they have been blind-sided by the tide.

'Stand up.'

This is the test. Either they will be spotted when they stand, or they will be free to move about at will. One by one they take courage and rise. They cannot see the ship. The ship cannot see them.

'Be quiet!' The jubilation of his men could undo them all.

He waits. Then:

'Bring up the horses.' Jeremiah heads back down the path – the rest follow their leader.

Customs house is a grand name for the building they are intending to rob. Its double doors look more imposing than they are and it's a moment's work for them to be kicked open. The noise of the attack reverberates, and they all stay rock still.

Nothing. Not only unsighted but too far away for sound as well. The wind is blowing from sea to shore tonight.

Encouraged, George leads the attack into the building, deep into the ground floor – he knows the revenue men will not have lugged his brandy and tea upstairs. The stash is quickly located; crow bars and axes make light work of liberating its contents.

'Make a chain!' he orders, and tea starts to come forward hand to hand, out through the doors to the horses waiting beyond. Each horse is loaded until it can take no more and then its rider heads for home. Thirty horses can manage the two tons of tea but only a little of the brandy. George knows he will not get a second chance. He is the last to leave – the only one with any of the precious spirit.

Once off the ridge they start to gallop, wanting distance between themselves and the customs house, even though it is unlikely the theft will be discovered until morning.

Word has spread like wildfire as the earliest riders have headed home, and people from the villages along the way come out to cheer them on. Any victory over the authorities is to be celebrated and smugglers are local heroes. They keep people supplied with cheap goods and these days almost everyone has a brother or cousin with more money in his pockets than he should have. George's men, flushed with victory, are buoyed by the attention and wave to anyone and everyone in the crowd.

Jeremiah Hardy goes further, spotting the shoemaker Daniel Challis who, like him, helped bring in the harvest last year. He plays to the crowd and greets Daniel warmly, leaning down to shake his hand, even reaching into one of his panniers to give him a packet of tea.

The caravan goes on its way. Challis basks in reflected glory. He shows everyone the tea; 'That was my friend Jeremiah Hardy' he tells anyone who will listen.

A small boast. One which will cost him his life.

Chapter 16

West Dean, Sussex
The Shoemaker's Shop
1739

'Mr Challis?'

The shoemaker looks up to see who is asking for him.

'You must come with me please.' William Barrow, a minor official in the revenue, is doing his best to be authoritative, but in truth he's not used to issuing orders. Like all the revenue men in the district he is employed by the Duke of Newcastle. He hasn't been doing the job for very long. Twenty-one last week and keen to impress.

Daniel Challis has never crossed swords with the law before. Barrow looks important to him, the uniform lending the young man what he lacks in himself – authority.

'Me? Why? Where to? I've orders to complete – I can't leave now.' Daniel cannot think of anything he has said or done which could have brought him to the attention of the authorities in this way. It must surely be a mistake.

'You have a friend called Jeremiah Hardy, Mr Challis?' Barrow starts gently, hoping the man will put up no resistance.

Challis puts down his last as he thinks about this. 'Jeremiah? Well, I know who he is, yes, but I'd hardly call him a friend.' Jeremiah Hardy is a smuggler and the subject of much current gossip. He was arrested and carried off some time ago – something to do with the raid on the customs house last year. Acknowledging him as a friend is not something it would be wise to do. Daniel himself is no smuggler and knows Jeremiah only through last year's harvest.

'Did he not shake hands with you and give you a packet of tea when he passed through here after the customs house raid?' Barrow knows the substance of the evidence the authorities have for Challis knowing Hardy quite well and puts it to him now.

'If he did, it was because I was there as he passed – not because I am a particular friend. We brought in the harvest together, which is as far as it goes.' Challis's mind is racing. Who has been talking?

'Calm yourself Mr Challis. You are not under suspicion of any wrongdoing yourself. But you are known to be able to identify Hardy to us and I am instructed to take you to Horsham to do exactly that. Nothing more will be required of you afterwards. Here – a letter from the Justice with those instructions.' Barrow offers the paper to Challis. Official documents are hard to deny. Even Barrow, inexperienced as he is, knows in the face of this letter Challis has no choice but to comply.

'I can't read sir. What is this? I've no wish to be involved – I'm no snitch. I won't do it.' He thinks Barrow looks unsure enough for him to be able to argue his way out of this, but he is mistaking inexperience for lack of will.

'Mr Challis. We have witnesses who saw you take a packet of tea from Hardy and shake his hand when the gang of rogues came through the village celebrating the raid. Do you deny it?'

Daniel knows he's in trouble; he let his tongue run off with his head when he boasted to anyone in the crowd who would listen, that Jeremiah was his friend. There must be dozens of people who can testify to this.

'If you won't help us Mr Challis, we will have to conclude you came by the tea in some other way – you were part of the raiding party. I think it would be an unfortunate conclusion, don't you?'

Unfortunate doesn't describe it. He has no wish to end up in the colonies.

'Please don't make me do this. I will be a marked man. I'm a shoemaker for God's sake. I mind my own business – let me be.'

Not yet hardened to heart-rending pleas for mercy, Barrow never the less reluctantly presses on.

'I'm sorry Mr Challis, I really am, but I have my orders. Come with me to Horsham and identify Hardy for us or come with me to Horsham and join him in gaol, whichever you prefer. Do you have a horse, or must I carry you on mine?'

Daniel has no choice. He considers trying to escape as he makes his way through the yard to collect his bay mare, but where would he go? His life and his business are here, though both will be ruined once he's known to be an informer.

Slowly he leads the animal round to the front of the house, mounts up, and sets off with Barrow for Horsham.

Chapter 17

Alfriston, Sussex
Bar of the Star Inn

Elizabeth Payne carries the last of the pots back into the Star Inn ready for the men coming in from the fields at noon.

She has been keeping the inn since her husband Jago was killed two years ago and is proud she is able to manage without needing either of her two sons to give up their smithing in the village to help her.

The pots are hardly stowed behind the bar before they arrive, followed by two strangers, one clearly a customs officer.

She has no immediate reason to fear him, she runs a good house, but she knows many of her customers are involved in smuggling and fears these two are a threat of some kind.

'What do they want?' She has watched this customer of hers, Peter Austin, talking to the men who joined him at his usual table in the window with their ales.

'Nothing to fear Liza – they're just taking a letter to Major Batten at the courthouse in Horsham and mean no-one here any harm. Leave them be.'

But Jago had been killed by a customs man in a raid gone wrong and she trusted none of them. Any letter they are carrying is likely to spell trouble for someone. Motioning to her eldest son to follow her, she goes outside.

'Go and fetch George Crawford, Clem, I don't like the look of those two in the window – fetch him here. They say they're taking a letter to Major Batten, but who knows what it means? George can decide whether it's safe to let them do it or not – Peter is far too trusting – he wouldn't recognise trouble until it was far too late to stop it.'

Clem follows his mother's gaze through the window to where Austin is still chatting happily to the two strangers who are gathering up their things as if to leave.

'Go, Clem, go now. I'll delay them somehow.'

'Could you have our horses brought round, mistress? We must continue on our way to Major Batten now that we have quenched our thirst.' William Barrow is anxious to complete his task. He never feels comfortable away from his fellow officers and is in a hurry to get back to them, whatever Daniel Challis decides to do when he gets to Horsham.

'Have another drink sir – there's no point hurrying. Major Batten will not be at home at this time of day. He'll be in town helping the schoolmaster. He'll be back mid-afternoon when the children come home.'

Elizabeth improvises as best she can. Barrow takes her at her word. He considers going into town to find the man, but the weather is hot and the ale good. He hands over his money and he and Challis go back to Peter Austin at the table in the window, content to wait a while longer.

Chapter 18

Alfriston, Sussex

The Star Inn

They're taking a letter to Major Batten in Horsham, George, but lord only knows what's in it.'

Crawford stands deep in thought.

'Bring the others inside.' This to Ned Payne, the younger blacksmith. To the elder: 'Get that fool Austin out of here Clem. He won't be needed.' Orders given, he returns to his drinking at the bar and waits until the strangers are alone.

'You're Daniel Challis, aren't you?' Crawford knows Challis from his visits to market in Fordingbridge. He knows he is a cobbler and can't think why he would be delivering letters to Henry Batten with a customs officer. It isn't yet a clear threat but it needs to be looked at. 'Could you come outside a moment – there's something I want to ask you.'

Challis, thinking himself on better terms with these local men than he is with the customs officer, follows him into the yard, but he's on no sort of terms with Crawford who is much better able to identify danger than the shoemaker.

George misses nothing. What he doesn't see, he is told. The name Daniel Challis has only been mentioned to him once recently, in connection with Jeremiah and some tea. It's the only link to the revenue he can think of, but it would be enough.

'Hardy, Jeremiah Hardy. He's disappeared – any idea where he is?' Poor Daniel. Crawford knows he has hit the target first time.

Challis senses the danger. 'Help me Mr Crawford, please get me away from here. Jeremiah is in custody in Horsham, as I think you know. When you all came through the village after the raid on the customs house, I took tea from him, and he called me friend. There are witnesses. This man Barrow is forcing me to go and identify him to the authorities. I have no choice but to do it. Help me – I must get away.'

'What are you doing out here Mr Challis?' Barrow comes into the yard to check that Daniel isn't trying to escape him.

'What's it to you?' Clem Payne has followed him out. The atmosphere is turning threatening.

George, in his youth, was an excellent poacher. He has tickled many a trout and knows jumping into things headlong is not always the best way to get things done.

'Steady Clem,' Crawford leads Challis back into the inn, followed by Barrow. 'These gentlemen are hot and tired – fetch them more ale and some rum and let them rest awhile.'

Back in the window, the outsiders are reassured as the ale and rum flow. Ned Payne and half a dozen other men slowly take up places at the bar. Eventually Crawford confronts Barrow.

'You carry a letter for Major Batten sir?'

'Indeed, I do, but what is it to you?'

'Show it to me please.'

Barrow has just enough sense left to deny this request, but not enough to realise it is not just an idle query. In fact the fearsome man asking for the letter attaches deadly importance to it, but neither the revenue man nor Daniel Challis can see this, fuddled as they are with all the free alcohol.

Crawford can see they are starting to lose their senses and instructs Elizabeth to keep the ale and rum flowing. Eventually, as intended, the alcohol has so much influence on Barrow and Challis that they succumb and nod off where they sit.

It is the work of a moment for George to search Barrow's bags and unearth the letter which confirms Daniel is, indeed, being taken to Horsham to do damage to their friend Hardy. If Hardy is convicted, he will almost certainly turn on them all.

'Burn it.'

Richard would not recognise his friend now – but he would know this cannot end well.

Challis and Barrow sleep on, surrounded by half a dozen angry and threatened men.

'Take them to the well and kill them.' Crawford issues the order but no-one moves. Killing people in a fight is one thing, to cold-bloodedly murder a customs officer in broad daylight is quite another.

'We can't do that, George. Too many of us have been seen with them and Mistress Payne has much to lose.' He knows this is right. He needs to be cleverer.

'We could take them to France on one of our next trips?' Thomas Jackson ventures a suggestion.

George considers this but rejects it very quickly. 'We could, but they could come straight back, identify us, and then where would we be?'

Elizabeth speaks quietly from the bar. 'Hang the dogs – they came here to hang you.' Her hatred is deep, with good reason.

'Why not keep them here until we find out what's happening to Jeremiah? If he goes free, so shall they.' George, in suggesting this, does not need to spell out the alternative.

Everyone already knows the two men's lives are hanging by a thread.

'Where will they be kept? They cannot lodge here – I have regular customers to look after.' Elizabeth does not want more trouble on her doorstep than there is already.

'Perhaps we should each give Mistress Page three pence a week for their keep.' This suggestion is met with universal disapproval. The change of mood is palpable. The men are angry now. Angry that they need to find a way of dealing with two men who are a direct threat to their livelihoods – and their lives – without further endangering themselves.

Enraged and frustrated, Thomas Jackson throws the two captives to the floor and drives his spurs into their foreheads to wake them, unable to contain himself any longer. 'Think you can harm Jeremiah Hardy and pay no price? By God, I'll make you pay!'

George, ever conscious of the mood of his men, makes his decision. He produces a horsewhip and wields it viciously, drawing blood. 'Come lads, let's have them out of here.' He pushes the two hostages towards the door where they are surrounded by others in the gang. He looks back to the bar.

'Say nothing of anything of this. If you do, I will shoot you myself.' They know this is no empty threat.

With that they are all gone.

Chapter 19

Alfriston, Sussex

Yard of the Star Inn

Out in the yard Barrow is trying to maintain some dignity and find his balance on the horse he is sharing with the shoemaker. He is facing Challis, their legs tied together under the stallion's belly. Up on Dandy, Crawford leads the party. The customs man and the shoemaker have no ability to influence the course of events from here. Barrow wonders where they are taking them. Have they any chance of escape?

'Whip 'em, cut 'em slash 'em, damn 'em!' comes Crawford's order. The blows come immediately, thick and fast. Barrow tries to hang on but it's not possible to withstand this kind of beating, especially not while trying to balance on the back of a horse tied to another man. Not far up the track he feels himself falling and braces for the landing but he is stopped short by the tethers which now keep him and Challis suspended under the beast, completely helpless.

'Pull them up straight!' Roughly they're pulled up and the dreadful journey starts again, the blows continuing until they fall, this time on the move, and are savagely struck by the horses' hooves as they go.

The train comes to a halt and Barrow hits the ground as the rope tethering him to Challis is cut. Both men are lifted roughly into the air, then thrown across the back of the horse, struggling to stay conscious. It would be more merciful if they were not aware of the utter humiliation which comes from being draped over a horse and having their genitals exposed for all to examine and poke, but even this small kindness is denied them.

On they go. The beating and mockery continuing all the way.

Neither man has any idea how far they have travelled when they are at last pulled to the ground.

'Throw them in the well!' comes the order.

Barrow is still sufficiently conscious to know that being abandoned in a well will mean a lingering death with no hope of discovery or rescue. He's had enough. 'For God's sake kill me now!' he pleads, but this is another terrible mistake.

'What have you done to deserve mercy?' Barrow can hear the fury in George's voice and knows from its tone his fate is set to get yet worse. He has no idea where Challis is and for the briefest moment regrets having forced the shoemaker to come with him to face what he now knows is certain death.

He is roughly pushed back up over the back of the horse and the dreadful journey, this time without Challis, starts again.

Chapter 20

South Downs, Sussex
At Lewis's Well

'Down on your knees and go to prayers, for with this knife I'll be your butcher.' George snarls at Daniel Challis who is no longer strong enough to be sent on horseback over the downs and lies cowering where he fell, close to Lewis's well.

He has sent Barrow away with his men, who have instructions to kill him when they can go no further, but Crawford has deep hatred for Challis who was ready to betray them all, even if he had no choice; he is beyond rational thought now.

Challis pulls himself up, kneels in front of George and begins to pray quietly. His predicament is so terrifying that he would be praying without any instruction from the bully who now has him at his mercy. He has no idea what has happened to the young customs man Barrow, but he hopes it's nothing good. Yesterday he was just an ordinary shoemaker. He thinks it is Barrow who has brought him to this but it was, in fact, done by his own hubris.

'You're an informing villain!' The kicking starts again and

Challis cannot stay upright for long as the blows rain down on his head.

'What have you done with Mr Barrow?' Challis is playing for time. He does not really need an answer to this question but asks as a desperate act of distraction. He really doesn't know his man.

From his belt, George draws his knife and holds it in front of him. Challis stares at it, hypnotised.

'Whatever we've done, you won't see it.' Crawford's knife slashes across Challis's eyes in a flash, almost cutting them out and removing most of his nose at the same time. 'You won't see anything again.' The second cut goes deep into his victim's forehead and Challis is quite sure this is the end. The man will surely stab him to death now.

He is mistaken. Lewis's well is thirty feet deep and no-one will find Challis there. Throwing him into it alive will be very satisfying. So would hanging him in it. George takes a rope from his saddlebag, forms a noose and puts it round Challis's neck, fastening the other end to the main strut of the well. 'Climb. Now. Get over.'

Challis, now blinded, can feel a wicker fence but has no clue what it can be guarding. Slowly he tries to climb but George, losing patience, pushes him over and he drops.

The rope is far too short for the drop to break his neck and he does not fall into the middle of the well but hits the side, which he clings to for dear life. It's not shock and pain making him weak now. Terror plays a much bigger part in it.

George considers his victim, braced against the edge of the well. Left there he will certainly die, slowly strangling to death. The man is so weak that it cannot take long, and Crawford has a fancy to watch it happen. He sits and waits, relishing the slowness of it, but after twenty minutes he realises he is putting himself in danger by staying so close to his prey. He cuts the rope and Challis disappears into the depths, still alive but with no hope of escape. George throws the wicker panels from the well onto the man below and follows these with a shower of the heaviest stones he can find. He keeps piling them on until the pleas for mercy stop.

He waits a while until he is sure he can hear nothing. And so, he goes.

Chapter 21

Bishopstone, Sussex
Richard and Jenny's Cabin
1740

Richard and Ann are sitting under a tree. He whittles a stick while she watches, wondering what delight he will fashion for her from this piece of wood and the small pile of others beside him. Pocketing his knife, he reaches for a pinecone and binds it to the top of the longest stick. Smaller ones are bound lower down and finally he holds out the doll to his precious girl. Something for her to hold on to when they go back to the house, and she discovers she is no longer their youngest child.

'Come Ann – I've another surprise for you.' He lifts her high onto his shoulders and she giggles. Her father is her world. High up behind his head with her new doll she couldn't be happier.

At the door Goodwife Brewer, who has come from Seaford specially, is waiting for him with James and Dickon. For a moment he is afraid – he has never forgotten how hard it was for Jenny the first time and has not been entirely comforted by people telling him that it gets easier each time.

'You have another son Richard – and yes, your wife is fine.' Mistress Brewer is old enough and wise enough to know she needs to reassure him about Jenny's safety as quickly as possible. But something in her face tells him this is not all she has to say. 'What? What is it? Is the child well – is he whole?'

'Yes, he's whole, and he has a tiny sister – you have twins! The two babes are with their mother inside.' She's a good woman but not one to face up to difficulties. She has spoken her own truth and is leaving it to Richard to find its meaning. 'Come James, come Dickon,' she takes the smallest boy's hand, 'let's take Ann to find some eggs in the village. You shall bring some home for your mother's tea.'

Richard carefully lifts Ann off his shoulders, all thoughts of showing her the baby forgotten. Something in the manner of the woman is not right, and she seems unusually keen to get the children away. 'Go with your brothers and the goodwife, Ann. I need to go and see your mother.'

Ann knows something has changed but she is too young to work out what. Her father is suddenly distant and sending her away. She's too sweet-natured to complain but doesn't leave willingly. She keeps turning back to her father as they go.

He watches them, deep in thought. How amazing. Twins; and Jenny well. But a shadow is forming; yet more mouths to feed and times are getting harder.

So distracted is he that he does not notice the few rough sticks he treads underfoot as he goes to meet his two new children; neither he nor Ann are thinking about the simple wooden doll anymore.

Inside, he finds Jenny sitting up, holding his new son and daughter. Neither is suckling and his wife stares at him blankly. He has never seen her like this before.

'They're both dead, Rich. There was nothing to be done. They're so tiny – they could not thrive. I didn't know there were two – I just thought I was a good size for one.' She is not crying. She is beyond it.

He looks at the three of them, helpless, and sinks onto the bed. Damn the goodwife. Why didn't she prepare him? 'Give me the boy.' The child is whole, as the woman had said, so so tiny in his perfectness, but still.

George is right. He is a fool. So busy worrying about danger to Jenny every time she gives birth he has never given a thought to the coming children. He tries to decide whether there was any sign of trouble this time but doesn't think so. Jenny has looked perfectly normal. Neither of them had known there were two babies. He doubts it would have turned out differently if they had.

Gently, he kisses the tiny cold head. The crib his father had made for James stands by the bed, waiting. Slowly he puts his third son in it and turns to his wife.

'Give her to me, Jen. Let her join her brother.'

She does not fight him.

In the gloom by a dwindling fire, they hold each other. Nothing to say. Nothing to do but wait.

In time the goodwife will return with the minister, and they will name the little ones Jude and Jane.

Richard need fear no more the two extra mouths to be fed.

Chapter 22

Bishopstone Place, Sussex
The Library

At Bishopstone Place, Newcastle is furiously angry again. After a hunt which lasted months, the body of William Barrow has been found on the downs, so badly beaten that only the remnants of his uniform identify him.

The Duke's anger does not come from any sort of sympathy for Barrow or his family. It comes from the pure frustration of being unable to stop gangs of smugglers doing whatever they like on his land. Enquiries have been made and he has known for some time Barrow was in the company of a shoemaker, Daniel Challis, on his way to Horsham to help the case against the gang which had embarrassingly emptied the customs house and reclaimed its confiscated goods.

It has taken weeks, but eventually Challis's body has also been found by chance at the bottom of Lewis's Well.

These murders are outrageous and simply cannot go unpunished. He's quite sure that most people in the area know who is responsible for the atrocities, but no-one is talking. Things in Sussex are getting out of control and it's felt for a long time as if the smugglers have the upper hand.

His mind has been working on the problem. Smugglers are preventing him from extracting the enormous income from his lands which should have followed enclosure and he has so far been unable to do anything to stop it.

It's time for Parliament to Act and Newcastle is slowly forming thoughts about the way it can be made to help.

He sighs deeply. What's the point of having a brother as prime minister if he cannot make use of him?

The time has come to call in the favour he is owed. He has long been the power behind the throne and Henry has been the principal beneficiary.

From his desk he writes:

My dear Henry

The smugglers are got to such an amazing height on the Sussex coast, that it has for some time become a very serious thing, and highly worthy of the consideration of Parliament.

Vast quantities of goods are being clandestinely imported in a triumphant manner, and the insults, menaces, and abuses given not only to the officers of the revenue, but to any other persons who offer to speak against their detestable practices are unimaginable.

The civil magistrates fully decline putting the laws in execution against them.

The insolence and outrageous behaviour of the smugglers has been, in my judgment, a public concern for some time, and calls loudly for Parliamentary redress.

They are a standing army of desperadoes, who pay themselves with their enormous profits, and subsist by no other means but public rapine and plunder.

If they cannot be broke, shut up Westminster Hall, and

disband all your officers of justice as an expensive but useless
encumbrance on the nation.

The terror which they spread makes Sussex a scene of horror
and confusion.

I remain, Sir,
Your loving brother,
Thomas

Henry must do something. And soon.

Chapter 23

Bishopstone, Sussex

Towards Newhaven
1742

Richard sits on the bank of the Ouse, hopefully dangling his line in the water. He is surprised to find himself happy. So much has happened to him in the last few years – his life is barely recognisable.

He and Jenny have settled into their new life in Bishopstone. Jenny has made a comfortable home for them in the delapidated cabin George has given them, though how she's done it he has no idea. She has been befriended by the minister's wife who has paid her a few pence every now and then to help at the vicarage with heavy work. She has made friends in the village and slowly a few bits of rough furniture have appeared, along with old but serviceable clothes for them all when people have taken pity on them and passed on what they can.

Many a man would mind such charity, but Richard sees it for what it is. Everyone loves his Jenny, and this is the result. The hardest thing about leaving Seaford was having to leave Mary Lucy in the graveyard there. Seaford's not very far away, and they visit, but he would rather have her sleeping close by as the twins do in Bishopstone churchyard.

His line goes suddenly taut, and he leaps to his feet. Through painful trial and error, he has learned how to land such a prize and soon there is a fat trout lapping on the bank which he regards with quiet pride.

He turns to pack and take his prize home to Jenny and sees James and Dickon running towards him, waving vigorously. 'Not more trouble, surely?' He lives in constant fear of something coming along to spoil their fragile new life, but he can see whatever it is they are coming to tell him, is nothing bad.

'Father, you must come at once. The goodwife is with mother – our new baby is coming today!' Dickon is shouting with excitement and Richard sweeps him into the air. He will need to be doing a lot more fishing as this family keeps growing but for today his trout is enough.

'Here James, carry this – we can make a fire outside and cook it for us all.'

The three of them begin the climb home. As he goes, he remembers all the other times, good and bad. This is the seventh, and as ever, he hopes it will be easy on Jenny.

He hasn't long to worry. The goodwife is leaving as they arrive. 'A bonny girl, Richard, and all's well. Jenny has already named her Elizabeth. Go in for yourself and see.'

Elizabeth. Their little Elizabeth.

She cannot be Mary Lucy, Jude or Jane but he will love her just the same, for the rest of his life.

Chapter 24

Bishopstone, Sussex

Between the Cabin and the Sea

Tired after a night awake with the new baby, Richard is glad to get out and back to fishing, though he will hardly admit it, even to himself. Halfway down to the river he sees a figure he knows well sitting on the grass, looking out to sea.

George is watching small ships out in the channel; sloops, cutters and luggers heading towards the mouth of the Ouse at Newhaven or a little further east towards Cuckmere Haven. They are a familiar sight to Richard who knows that these days smugglers don't even wait till night to bring their goods in to shore – they have an apparently free hand. He sees them almost every day while he is fishing, understanding what they're at, but doesn't give it much thought.

He knows, of course, but does not want to openly admit, that George comes here to watch for his own cargoes arriving. Sometimes he comes to this spot to watch the traffic going the other way to France, having raced up from the creek once his small boats are loaded and pushed out to sea.

Their cabin on the way to Bishopstone is a reasonable

excuse for George to be here if anyone is interested enough to ask. Why wouldn't he be visiting his friends and godchild?

'Good morning, George, you're early.' Richard wonders if he has heard about the new baby and come to wish them well. 'You've heard about our new child?'

George gets to his feet, shaking his head. 'No – so soon? Boy or a maid?'

'Maid. Elizabeth. I'm in no hurry to start this morning, she gave me no sleep! Come back with me now and see her with Jenny.'

George shakes his head. 'Not this morning Rich. Jenny will be wanting her rest. But congratulations man – sit with me a while and tell me all about it.'

His eyes return to the sea and Richard can tell he is not just idly watching the boats come and go. He's here for a reason that has nothing to do with friendship.

Richard sits next to the man who has been like father or brother to him for so long. Both look out to sea. It's hard to miss the much larger ship anchored far out on the horizon – an East India vessel most likely – or the flurry of smaller ships heading towards it like bees to blossom.

It's no coincidence George is here today. This is one of his biggest cargos – all the way from China. He is now so established that he can deal, without danger, with friends at the East India Company in London who can make the odd boat go astray at will in return for a share of the proceeds.

Richard and George do not mention the big boat, each knowing it is best kept unacknowledged by either of them if George is connected to it. In his wildest dreams Richard still does not suspect the full extent of George's involvement in Sussex smuggling. The Lewes house speaks of increasing wealth, but Richard, simple soul, thinks this somehow comes from a few small sheep raids and maybe a bit of tea dealing here and there.

George wonders what his friend would think if he knew everything they are watching is happening because of him. All the little boats, all the men in them – all his. The cargo being unloaded from the East Indiaman – also his, bought and paid for in London several months ago.

He does not think the smuggling of wool, tea, brandy and the rest would be a big surprise or problem for his friend. It's what goes with it. He has risen to the top of this tree by unimaginably ugly means, and he knows both Richard and Jenny could not look up to him and rely on him in the way they do if they suspected even the half of it. They, like everyone else in Sussex, know the smugglers are led by the man who calls himself Black Diamond, but no-one outside the gangs know who this is. He is determined; neither of his friends will ever discover the truth.

So they sit, the friends, watching the activity at sea. In the early days, long before Richard and Jenny came here, George often sat in this spot for days on end, waiting for a signal from the sea. He did the same thing on Seaford Head on their wedding day, he remembers, but as part of a small gang, not leader of the whole Sussex network.

'We are happy here George.'

'I'm glad. But I could do much more for you, you know.'

'I do, but I'm content. I've told you before – your way of life is not for me. Some heavy work on the reservoir and then some fishing is a perfect life for me, and we manage to get by on it, which is all I ask. Call in to Jenny before you leave – she'll be glad to see you.'

He's not absolutely sure she will. When he talks about George these days, he senses a caution in her. The carefree days they all spent together in times past do not happen now.

He suspects that Jenny, listening to Dodo, has heard more of George's life than she has shared with him, and he has not encouraged her to tell him what she's learned. He is saddened, but his love for George is as strong as it ever was. He sets off down the path to the creek, giving a cheerful salute as he goes.

George watches him, deep in thought. Once he thought Richard a fool for not joining him. He does not do so now. He does not like himself, the life he leads, does not like who he has had to become. The simple honest life of Richard touches a part of him so deep he hardly knows it's there.

No way back for him. His path is much, much darker.

Chapter 25

Houghton Hall, Norfolk
The Red Saloon
1744

At Houghton Hall, Walpole is surrounded by guests. Newcastle, his brother Henry Pelham the Prime Minister (the King was right, and it still hurts, but it pays to be pragmatic), Weaving and Castle, influential tea dealers both, and the very interesting Widow Kesteven whose coffee house has lately gone from strength to strength in St James and recently began selling brandy and rum along with the coffee.

'The smuggling business simply cannot be allowed to go on.' Newcastle addresses Pelham, sitting opposite. 'I have told you time and again these gangs are running riot all over Sussex. You have to make it stop.'

'What would you have me do?' Pelham looks round the room, genuinely perplexed.

Walpole decides it's finally time to enlighten him. 'I have asked these gentlemen – and this lady – to join us because I think they have a great part to play in the solution to this problem.' He nods toward Weaving, Castle and the Widow Kesteven.

Weaving is clearly affronted. His dealings with smugglers

are both lucrative and discreet and any public accusation of a connection between himself and smuggling is something he will fervently deny, however inaccurate such a denial might be.

'We sir? Whatever do you mean? I cannot think of anything we can do to stop the rascals – we are merchants, not brigands.'

'No indeed. You are respectable London merchants one and all, but come, let's not pretend your success in recent years doesn't rest largely on your use of illegal untaxed supplies of tea, coffee and alcohol.' Walpole, already out to grass, has nothing to lose by making this assertion openly.

The Widow Kesteven smiles, her nod almost an assent. 'Profit must come from somewhere sir – and taxed goods leave us nowhere to turn. If people cannot drink their coffee and brandy at a reasonable price in my house, they will certainly frequent places elsewhere where they can.'

'Indeed Madam.' Walpole also nods. 'But your enterprises are much larger than those other, smaller places. It follows that your profits are of an order so large those little traders can never reach them. You three were in it at the start and have balance sheets to show just how much you have taken from the mayhem our friend Newcastle has described. You do not involve yourself in any of it, I'm quite sure, but turning a blind eye and taking the goods is, in the view of some, just as culpable.'

'Really sir!' Weaving almost gets to his feet. 'Withdraw that remark. It's unseemly, especially addressed to a lady.'

'Calm yourself Weaving,' the Widow smiles as she encourages him back into his chair. 'Unseemly, perhaps, but not lacking in truth.' She turns to Pelham. 'The answer is in your hands sir. We would not be buying from smugglers – if we do – were the taxed supplies available to us at equal or similar price to theirs.'

'What on earth do you mean?' Pelham, never as sharp as his brother, does not grasp the full meaning of her words.

'Quite simply, sir, you must cut your taxes.'

Newcastle looks from one end of the table to the other as what she has said sinks in. Eventually, showing no emotion, he says: 'It's a novel idea and a very interesting one at that.' He gives no sign the idea is his, a solution so clever even he is still surprised when he hears it.

Pelham looks aghast. The merchants are unreadable.

The contribution from Widow Kesteven has been more than enough for them, not having been given any warning of what was afoot. Walpole, ever the pragmatist and, though no-one admits it, still a power behind the throne, looks to Pelham.

'Why not? It must surely be worth considering. I know from the treasury how steeply revenues have declined in the last several years as more and more people find easy access to supplies of untaxed goods. Surely it must be worth calculating how much of the missing revenue can be regained from selling goods at a radically lower tax rate?'

'A lower tax rate? No one lowers tax rates, not when revenue is falling!' Pelham does not see how this can be a genuine suggestion and half wonders if he is being teased.

His brother is quick to step in. 'Maybe that's exactly when the rate should be cut, Henry. You should cut to the point where the smugglers can barely match the official rate and they will be forced out of business. It will be the end of them.'

'You'd need to cut by at least seventy eight percent.' Weaving realises immediately he has given himself away and looks sheepish, but he has been calculating rapidly. He has been forced to admit openly he knows the precise size of the gap between his two sets of available suppliers. Nobody is surprised. It's a game they play – never admit to knowing a smuggler – and they all stick by the rules.

'The revenue at present charges me four and nine pence in the pound on bonded tea and the same for all other goods. My guess is the smugglers – a very sophisticated bunch at the top I understand – mark up by, say, twenty five percent when they sell in London to be able to take their cut.'

'Well, they have expenses to pay, I suppose, just like the rest of us.' Castle puts in, giving himself away, if anyone were interested, as he does so.

Weaving presses on with his point. 'I may be wrong – better brains than mine will have to check – but, as I say, I think you have to cut the tax by seventy eight percent or so to match the smugglers' prices.'

They don't need to check. Weaving makes his living buying and selling – his calculation is too low by just under one per cent. Walpole and Newcastle already know this. Only Pelham is surprised.

'Seventy eight percent! Are you mad sir?' Pelham cannot grasp any of it.

Walpole turns to Newcastle.

'Do you think it may be worth exploring? Nothing more.'

'Indeed. There's no doubt high duty on these goods has allowed smugglers a lot of room for manoeuvre and enabled them to undercut the sellers of bonded goods. This has given the smugglers so much profit even the lowliest of them are paid uncommon well. Half a guinea a journey is the going rate in Sussex, I'm told, topped up with a dollop of tea. Enough to tempt even the most industrious and honest labourer to the cause.'

'Half a guinea a journey per man? But there can be two or three hundred of them on the big raids – a small fortune!' Pelham begins to reckon his government's losses. It's a start.

'If that's what the meanest are paid from their twenty five percent, how much is going to the men at the top? Add it all up and put it into your revenues and you will be very surprised, I think. Why not let the treasury do some work on the likely effects of a twenty percent, fifty percent and seventy five percent cut on taxes, on the proviso that the final amount will bring the goods down to the level being offered to these honest traders – he bows to Weaving, Castle and the Widow – by their alternative suppliers at present?' Newcastle looks to Pelham and waits.

'I cannot see it will do harm to find out.' Grudgingly Pelham turns to the merchants. 'This will need your co-operation. The treasury must know your cost prices and how much you are selling before they can make any sensible estimations.'

The three return his gaze. There is a pause and then:

'Were we to give you any information, we must be guaranteed immunity from prosecution if it were to become evident any of us has dealt with smugglers.' Castle's demand is made softly, but its import is enormous.

Newcastle and Walpole wait. They have worked towards just such an outcome for many months. Nothing has been said which has come as a surprise to either of them.

'Henry?'

'We simply can't do that. Very few people are granted immunity from prosecution and in this case, you could be talking of hundreds of people.' His knowledge of the scope of deals being done with smugglers is, thus, also laid bare.

'Seriously Henry. You know we have sought a solution to this problem for months, if not years. I can see no other way.'

Pelham comes under the gaze of both his predecessor and his sponsor. He knows there is no escape.

'Very well.'

Turning to the merchants he mutters 'you have my word as Prime Minister; in return for the information you provide about your dealings with smugglers you will be granted immunity from prosecution for crimes disclosed as part of the investigation.'

And so the world turns. Another deal is done.

The deal has been brokered in the best interests of everyone involved in the making of it. Of course. How could it be any other way?

Chapter 26

Holborn, London
The Nag's Head
1745

Away from the hustle of the public bar at the Nag's Head in Holborn, George Crawford waits in his room overlooking the courtyard.

He regularly stays at this old inn on his trips up from Sussex. He comes for many reasons. Most of his goods are held in his warehouses in Stockwell, but lesser amounts are brought here, later to be sent out across the capital in parcels. His duffers can each carry up to a quarter hundred weight of tea on foot. They carry it all over London, selling to hawkers as they go, bringing the proceeds back to the Nag's Head where it is lodged behind the bar for George to collect when he arrives.

He needs to be seen regularly by these men. He is formidable, and it does no harm to remind them whose goods they carry. He comes mainly to be seen by them, but while he is here, he is also able to meet his most valued customers; then, on the way home, he can call into his warehouses in Stockwell which hold the bulk of his wealth and need careful watching.

This evening George is nervous. Earlier in the day he has met with Weaving, then Castle and finally, the Widow

Kesteven at their various establishments in Knightsbridge. He has sold them 2,000, 1,000 and 2,000lbs of tea respectively which he will see delivered from Stockwell in the depths of tonight before returning to Sussex at dawn. Nothing unusual here – he does this every ten days or so.

But something unusual has happened today. Their deal concluded, Weaving took him aside and begged to be allowed to visit him in Holborn this evening. He did not indicate why he should want to do such an extraordinary thing but stressed the matter was urgent. Usually, the London merchants go out of their way not to be seen with him.

Rooms at the Nag's Head are above the stables and, shortly before seven, Weaving can be heard climbing the staircase from the yard. George ushers him into his room and checks there are no witnesses – neither wants to be seen meeting here.

'Well Weaving – what brings you here of all places? Could you not have spoken to me this morning when we met – or tonight when we meet again?'

Weaving grasps George's arm and hisses urgently; 'I have news Mr Crawford, news of a plot to stop you in your trade, which I think may very well succeed.'

George is not yet alarmed but his mind goes straight to betrayal.

'Stop me? How? Which of my men is plotting against me?' George, having climbed the greasy smuggling pole himself, is ever on the look-out for threats from his men.

'Not just you sir, all of your kind. And it's nobody's man sir – it's the government.'

The relief shows plainly on George's face. The government does not have the manpower to stop his, or anyone else's operation without using the army and he knows there would be no support for that. People in villages up and down the land make a very comfortable living by helping him in his enterprises and they will not walk away from money and cheap goods easily.

'I'd like to see them try,' his laughter is loud, and genuine. 'They cannot take us on without provoking rebellion. There are too many of us and we have the support of the common people.'

He is very confident in this, and he is correct. He has not considered, though, what would happen to support if the money dried up.

'No George. They won't be stopping you physically. A deal has been struck – I won't say by whom – and the revenue on coffee, tea, brandy and all other bonded goods will shortly be cut by Act of Parliament from four and nine pence in the pound to just one single shilling. It will bring the selling price of those goods well within the reach of yours, if not lower. You will no longer have customers, even loyal ones such as myself, because they will no longer need you. I have always disliked trading illegally, but the money was right. This will allow me to come back within the law.'

George is taken completely by surprise. The possibility of such action has no more crossed his mind than it had Henry Pelham's. It's clever and he wonders who it was who thought of it. He knows straight away it will work. His brain is razor-sharp, which is why he's been so successful. He sees no way out of this if it's true.

'When does it happen?'

'The Act is going through Parliament next week. Its effect will be immediate.' Weaving is so definite about it that George doesn't doubt it for a minute. Stunned, he sinks back onto the settle. So soon. The end will come so soon. Not of everything; there will always be money to be made from small local operations on the coast, but the trading on which his fortune rests is doomed if Weaving is correct.

Weaving though. Something more must be in it for him,

otherwise he would not have come with this warning. He would just have waited for the Act to go through.

'Why do you tell me this?' He does not expect a straight answer from Weaving but the force of his presence provokes one.

'Your warehouses in Stockwell –' Weaving hesitates, then plunges on. 'I am authorised by my fellows to buy all your stock at cost to get it off your hands. You cannot clear much of it any other way and we have the ability to get it out onto the market without drawing undue attention to ourselves.' He has the good grace to look uncomfortable as he makes this offer, which is, in truth, an ultimatum from on high.

George makes a play for time. 'It will take months for everything to come through. I have ships on their way from India with cargo bound for you and dozens of others.'

'Fine. We will continue to buy from you until every pound or dram has made its way to Stockwell. Then you will shut it down.'

There it is then. Shut down his entire operation. If he turns down Weaving's offer the value of all his stocks will be lost by the end of next month; he doesn't doubt the authorities know exactly where they are. This way he will at least be able to realise his assets over a reasonable length of time.

The confident way the offer has been made confirms that it comes with tacit approval from someone in authority. A blind eye will be turned to this continuance of trade – in return for what?

'How do I know you speak truth?'

Weaving has recovered. He has just forced through a substantial deal – George has been given no choice.

The government may be greatly reducing Weaving's own profit margins with the new Act, but this deal guarantees a few more month's cheap supplies so he can continue to undercut his smaller rivals. All this and guaranteed government immunity from prosecution for illicit trading, past, present and future.

'I tell you no lie George. Wait and it will be too late. There would be no benefit in me making up such a tale. The bill passes very soon.'

George, defeated and floored by the unexpectedness of it all, gives a shrug.

'So be it. We will empty the Stockwell warehouses as fast as we can.'

He does not hear Weaving leave.

Chapter 27

Cuckmere Haven, Sussex

Between the Cabin and the Shore
1746

Richard is on his way to go fishing. The day is bright and clear, and he can see boats coming in – too many to count. Something unusual is happening. The activity has an urgency about it which disturbs him. He knows George is there and suddenly has an overwhelming urge to see him, so passes his regular fishing spot and continues to the shore. He could not tell anyone, if asked, why he does this; he doesn't know, he just senses need.

He finds George wrestling with a brandy barrel coming off the last boat. There is a sad desperation about him Richard has not seen before.

'What's happening George?'

All pretence between them is lost. 'This is my last big cargo, Rich. It has cost me dear and if I am to be paid for it, I must get it to London tonight.'

Richard can see George, always so sure and strong, is really struggling. He takes one end of the barrel, and they make their way upriver towards the headland where it can be loaded onto whatever transport must be waiting to take it to London.

As they crest the hill, he is amazed to find thirty or forty mounted horsemen, obviously waiting for instructions from George, who Richard finally realises must be their leader, the infamous Black Diamond.

Richard wonders how he did not know this or, rather, with sudden insight, why he did not let himself know this?'

George begins to lash the last barrel to Dandy while Richard watches sadly. He can no longer pretend he doesn't know how important George is – it's all too obvious.

Suddenly, from a stand of trees to the east, a troop of horsemen, all wearing customs uniforms, breaks cover, their intention clearly to intercept the gang as it heads to South Lane and then onto the London Road.

George, survival instinct honed and intact, runs for cover, leaving Richard and Dandy as he goes. Richard, never having been in any trouble in his life, does not react. There is nowhere he can go with the animal, so he takes its bridle to stop it running off and stands with it, stroking its nose, sensing no danger to himself in what is happening.

The officers spread themselves across the road. 'What are you carrying boys? We need to take a look – is that a problem?'

A rough-looking man, who Richard has never seen before, pulls a pistol from his coat and starts firing into the air to frighten the officers away. Dandy is startled by this and Richard struggles to hold him, calming him as best he can, very unsettled himself at this unexpected turn of events.

'We'll blow your brains out if you attempt to seize anything here!' yells the man. A great cry and hullabaloo start up from the others and more shots are fired, though Richard cannot tell where, or who, they come from.

'We'll have your cargo if you please sirs.' The officer is undaunted and, dismounting, takes his sword, and cuts bags of tea and several half anchors of brandy from the lead horse.

All hell breaks loose. 'Save the cargo! Save the cargo!' is the cry from George's men. 'Drive the horses away. Stand firm and shoot them dead!'

The horses and their cargo are driven away, while the gang stands resolutely between them and the officers.

Without evidence the revenue men know they will not be getting much reward today. It is all slipping away from them.

Throughout all this Richard holds Dandy, still laden with George's brandy. If the officers get the barrel, George will be in trouble because everyone knows this is George's horse. Richard loves him too much to let that happen. He slips the halter over the animal's head and slaps its flank, driving it off to follow the others which are heading over the hill at speed.

One officer looks hard at Richard, who is left holding only the halter. He will surely know him again.

The gang, satisfied there is nothing they can be caught with to incriminate them, starts to run in all directions.

Richard watches them go, left alone with the halter. He must not keep it – it links him to the smugglers. He begins to understand the peril he is in and finally throws it down. The customs officers are distracted by all the men running away and take no notice of Richard; he looks back to the place where George disappeared and, finally, runs for his life.

Chapter 28

Kensington Palace, London
The Orangery

'I need help in the North.'

'Help, your Majesty – with what?' though Newcastle knows perfectly well. Support for James Stuart in the north has been steadily rising and it cannot be long before it turns south for war. The naval blockade off Sussex has so far succeeded in stopping supporters of the rebels rampaging their way across his lands on their way to join the Pretender's army when it strikes, but it can't last forever.

'Jacobite rising they're calling it – Charles is raising an army in Scotland to come and take my throne for James. It cannot be allowed.'

'Then fight it, sire.' As things stand, Newcastle knows King George has no hope of doing any fighting. His armies are still in Europe winding down the war of Austrian succession, though no-one, least of all the King, really knows why they're still there. Any rebellion at home, north or south, will not be easily fought off.

'I must have men to fight in Scotland. I believe you have plenty who could fight for me?'

'I have my own men, yes – and could muster many more. But I'm not quite sure why I would.'

Newcastle the arch manoeuverer disingenuously makes his first move. Having secured the enclosure of his lands in Sussex, he has only two remaining problems. Properly handled this conversation will allow him to solve both in one go.

First, helping the king overcome the Jacobite rebellion will stop any question of French troops invading Sussex on their way north. Second, the King will be forced, in return, to give him what he came seeking today. In that case his lands will become truly his own, no longer threatened by invaders or constantly upended by marauding hordes of smugglers.

'What is your price?' The King cuts straight to the chase. He is weary and wants this over quickly.

'My principal desire, as ever, is to see the end of smuggling across my lands. Sussex is still in thrall to these villains, and I want it stopped.'

'But Pelham tells me the new revenues will bring it all to a halt very quickly. Surely that satisfies you?' The King doubts this. He has known Newcastle for a very long time. He knows nothing will ever satisfy him. There will always be further demands.

'No, sire, it does not. They will continue to run fast and loose all over Sussex even if they cannot get high prices in London anymore. Enough local landlords will buy from them to make it worth their while to continue.'

The king's patience is wearing thin. 'Then what do you suggest Newcastle? I would not be asking for help with a rebellion today if I had men to spare to deal with these malevolent gangs.'

'No, sire. They are too many and too brutal for that. But I suggest such brutality should be met with brutality. They must be treated in a language they understand – death.'

112

'Death?' He hadn't expected this. He has never understood the visceral cruelty of the English; it always surprises him how quickly they turn to it.

'Yes, sire, death. I want anyone convicted of smuggling – or even of consorting with smugglers – to find themselves automatically on the end of a rope, which would make everyone else think twice before carrying on.'

'But surely they already know they risk spending the rest of their lives in the colonies or somewhere equally dreadful. Is that not enough to make them stop and think?'

'Apparently not. If you want me to raise an army for you to go north, my price is an Act of Parliament making death certain for any smuggler, or known associate of a smuggler, who is taken.'

'Is that all?' The King's sarcasm in response to the gruesome nature of this request goes unnoticed.

'No. There's more. If these villains are to be caught, we need to stop the local populace protecting them. They must be given up. We must offer a reward of £500 to anyone who causes a smuggler to be captured.'

'£500? A fortune! Are you sure about this? How can it be justified?'

'I am very sure, sire. £500 is a sum large enough to change lives, enough to loosen the most loyal tongues. It will be paid to an informer exactly a month to the day after the man he has found for us hangs. And hang he will – the law should allow no appeal.'

He is deadly serious. The King knows Newcastle of old. He is a skilled politician who understands exactly how to get what he wants; who never makes a request without knowing he has his opponent trapped in a position that makes it impossible to refuse.

Gracious concession is the only option here.

'Very well Newcastle. I shall get Pelham to see to it immediately.'

Newcastle remains impassive.

'Thank you, your majesty.' A slight bow. 'Now, let's talk about your army.'

Chapter 29

Bishopstone Place, Sussex
The Knot Garden
1747

Newcastle is content. A year ago the Jacobite rebellion was crushed at Culloden which means there is no longer any threat to his lands of invasion. Two new laws have safely passed through Parliament, one lowering taxes, the other making it impossible to befriend smugglers; these will surely solve his problems in Sussex. He and Richmond walk the grounds at Bishopstone Place, happy with what has been done.

'We have our wish – the Acts have passed into law. What happens now?' Richmond is interested to know how Newcastle intends all this to play out. He does not deceive himself into thinking he has made any contribution to the plan.

'The quickest way to get people to understand the effect of a law is to put it into practice,' comes the reply. 'We need a hanging.'

'Yes, indeed, a big one.' Richmond wonders how such an event will affect his influential London circle, many of whom have traded and been friends with the most important smugglers for years. Newcastle appears to have no such concern, but then, his lands are far more extensive than Richmond's and there is more money at stake for him.

'No Charles. A small one, preferably a local man.'

Richmond heaves a sigh of relief but does not really see where this is going.

'We cannot hang a big fish. Were they not so untouchable, smuggling would have been over long ago. We need someone small, someone from Sussex who no-one would expect to hang, someone no-one in London will know or have heard of. Such a hanging will send a powerful message to the whole of Sussex. If it can happen to the smallest fish it can happen to anyone.'

The brilliance of it slowly dawns on Richmond. No-one, he ruefully reflects, should ever underestimate Newcastle.

'I see. Yes, I see. We need someone to be an example. How do we find such a man?'

'I have already spoken to the magistrates.'

Chapter 30

Bishopstone, Sussex
Richard and Jenny's Cabin

Richard and Jenny tend the fire outside the cabin, waiting for their evening fish to be ready. Squeals of delight from the children tell of great fun being had close by.

'What is it Rich?' Jenny knows her husband well and can see he is not as happy as she is this evening. She has everything she wants – her home, a good man, four happy children and another on the way.

'Where is George, Jenny? It's as if he never was. It's four months since the raid and no-one has set eyes on him.'

'He's lying low, and why wouldn't he? If he's Black Diamond as you suspect, he'll have a high price on his head.' Her face darkens. 'How could he have endangered us so? If he is really so important, he was bringing trouble to our door every time he came near. I thought him so kind when he brought us here, but now I think we were just being put to good use by him.'

Richard, whatever his suspicions, still cannot bear to hear Jenny speak badly of George, his oldest and dearest friend.

'Don't say so. He never asked anything of us in return for this place. Yes, we could have been lookouts from here – it's perfectly placed I grant you – but he never asked us to do it.'

'He never had the need. The time would have come, I'm quite sure.' Jenny is much less forgiving than her husband and, like almost everyone who has been duped, bitter. So bitter at the moment, she hopes she never sets eyes on George again.

'We don't know that Jen. I miss him – where can he be?'

'Hiding in his tunnels like the rat he is. There are enough of them as you should know.' Richard had not enjoyed his time tunnelling under George's house in Lewes and had, indeed, come to know rats very well in the process.

Suddenly they hear horses approaching. Exchanging a puzzled look, they get to their feet and wait, Richard's arm instinctively protecting his wife and unborn child. Three customs officers dismount and stride purposefully towards them.

'Richard Ashcroft?'

'Yes sir.' He answers with an open face – these men are officers of the law. He is an honest man. They cannot be any threat to him.

'We have a warrant for your arrest for smuggling offences sir – I'm afraid you must come with us.'

The shock on Richard's face is obvious. He scarcely understands what has just been said. 'Smuggling? Me? No sir. I am a fisherman – ask anyone round here. There is some mistake.'

'There is no mistake. You were part of the raid last September not far from here – I saw you there myself.' Richard looks at the man and remembers him watching him closely on the night he last saw George Crawford. There is no point denying he was there.

The customs officer knows he has his man. He studied

Richard on the day. All the men had been familiar to him except this one, who had behaved oddly and been in no hurry to get away, which had not, unfortunately, given the officer pause for thought. Others, recently arrested, had named Richard and sealed his fate, hoping to make their fortunes and save themselves in the process.

'We have been looking for you for months and your whereabouts have lately been reported to us. I am arresting you on suspicion of smuggling and you must come with us straight away. Do not make us take action we might all regret.' The pistol is quietly taken from under the officer's coat to make it clear this is no joke.

Richard gives Jenny a hug. 'Don't worry Jenny – there is some mistake here about what I did in the raid. I shall go with these men and get it sorted out.' He disappears inside to collect what few things he has that may be of use to him while he's away.

'Where are you taking him?' Jenny is becoming distraught. She and Richard have never been apart. They rely on him for food – for everything. Her friends from the village will not help her if they think her husband is a criminal.

'We must take him to the assizes in Horsham, ma'am. You are free to visit him there.' Looking around he can see no horse, so knows such a journey cannot be made by her – especially given the size of her belly. He wonders what happened to the horse Richard had been holding during the raid. It had been a fine animal; not one he would have expected to come from here.

'Please don't take my husband!' She is desperate now and, on her knees, begging. 'He's a good man – there is some dreadful mistake.' The customs officer looks down on her; 'Funny. That's what they all say.'

Richard comes out with his pitifully small bundle. He does

not try to resist arrest; he knows he could not succeed, but in fact sees no reason to resist. Jenny is right. There is a mistake. All will be put right in Horsham.

Chapter 31

Horsham, Sussex
The Magistrate's Court

'This man should not be here.' Giles Barnaby is the youngest of the three magistrates deliberating on Richard's fate. It seemed to Giles that what they had heard this morning had been very thin evidence of the man's guilt. Now they must decide whether he should be tried for smuggling under the new law or not. The recent changes make this a heavier duty than it used to be. Certain death awaits anyone found guilty on such a charge.

'I agree.' Hugo Morton, the second magistrate, wants his dinner. Dismissing the charge won't take long. 'The man is far too soft to be what they purport him to be. There is no arrogance in him, and he appears to have a touching faith in the law; not something I see in the smugglers who regularly appear before me. I don't know what happened here – he was certainly there, he says so, but the consequence of any decision by us to send him to trial would weigh heavily on me. I suggest we reprimand him for keeping bad company and send him back to his wife and fish.'

'No sirs. He must go to trial.' William Gorringe, the senior magistrate, is adamant. Unusually so. He is known locally to be a fair man and his colleagues would not have expected him to take this line. Barnaby looks questioningly at him. Something is going on under the surface here.

'William? The case is thin. Why risk a man's life on it? Yes, he has declared himself guilty of being there, but there is no evidence at all of him smuggling.'

'We are not asked to judge the case today, nor to decide whether he is a smuggler. We must simply agree to send him to trial. The thinness or otherwise of the evidence is for a jury to review. I say he goes to trial.' Something in his manner says he will brook no opposition.

'We must simply agree to send him to trial? There's an alternative surely. Why do you say this so decisively?' Barnaby probes the statement which feels odd to him.

Gorringe does not intend to enter into debate. 'Because it's what I know we must do.' Indeed he does.

Hugo really wants his lunch. 'Well, if you say so, then I will agree to it, but I think it harsh.'

William is not about to care whether this decision is harsh. His recent elevation to friendship with The Duke of Newcastle, cemented over dinner at Bishopstone Place, has put him on the lookout for just such a man as Richard; a local man who can be tried for smuggling, but unexpectedly so. Someone with a hitherto unblemished reputation. A perfect scapegoat.

They have finished conferring. The decision is made.

'The prisoner will stand.'

Richard rises. He will be back with Jenny tonight.

'We find the case against the prisoner strong enough for him to go to trial.'

Gorringe hesitates now. He knows he must do what he is about to do, because it has been very carefully explained to him over excellent salmon by the Duke. Climbing the greasy pole can be hard. It involves unsavoury things. He draws breath but does not look at Richard, keeping his eyes instead on the papers in front of him.

'Richard Ashcroft. The charge against you is so heinous, the evidence so strong, that we do not believe this case can be tried sufficiently well here in Horsham. You will be sent immediately to Newgate prison in London – there to await trial at the Old Bailey Sessions at the earliest available date.'

The gasps of disbelief from the court – the heads of William's companions snapping to look at him in astonishment – all are lost on Richard.

He's going to London. He will not see Jenny tonight.

How is this happening to him?

Chapter 32

Horsham, Sussex
The London Road

Outside the courthouse George is waiting. When he first heard of the arrest, he had been sure nothing untoward could come of it – he, more than anyone else, knew for certain Richard had done nothing that should keep him away from his family for more than a few months at most.

He is here to take his friend home – it would be a very long walk otherwise.

A cart draws up with six hefty men on board. They, too, wait. Well back in the trees, he watches in mounting disbelief as Richard is brought out, obviously not a free man. What's happened here?

He sees him hoisted onto the cart and surrounded by the six men, who must have been ordered here in advance, charged with guarding him. Someone knew, then, what the verdict would be. George continues to watch as the cart heads up the London Road at speed. It's going the wrong way surely?

It makes no sense and, although he knows himself to be a wanted man, George risks approaching the officer who brought Richard out of the court. This far away from Lewes and

Seaford, in his guise as a man about town, he reckons he is very unlikely to be recognised. He's right. To the officer of the court the appearance and manner of the man approaching him is that of a gentleman.

'What has happened to the man in the cart? Where is he going?' There is authority in his voice; it's a part he has often played and he slips into it well.

'He's signed his own death warrant is what's happened to him, sir' comes the abrupt reply.

'His death warrant? For what? What can you mean?' George is shaken and needs an answer.

'He has admitted being in the company of smugglers September last, although he says he is no smuggler himself.'

'Nor he is – I can vouch for that.' He's throwing caution to the wind here, but the officer does not stop to wonder how he can be so sure of his ground. 'Why is he being taken away for being with smugglers? What law has he broken if he is not one himself?'

'Have you not heard? The law has changed sir. Anyone who keeps company with smugglers while they're smuggling these days is condemned to death without question. A man no longer has to be a smuggler to die – he just has to admit he was near one during a raid, and that man just did.'

'Law – what law? When did it change?' How has he missed this? If something has happened to put Richard of all people in danger of the rope, then he and all his men are in great peril – and their families too, if this right.

'Two months back. Smugglers caught in the act, or anyone in their company while they're doing it, are guilty straight away – and it's death now – not the colonies!'

All the calculations George has made about his way of life turn to dust. The assumption that, with help from influential customers at trial, there was a good chance of escaping death and starting a new life overseas had underpinned his determination to keep going. It was the same for all his men.

But the officer hasn't finished.

'Do you know any smugglers sir?'

The man has been completely fooled by the clothes George wears for mixing with his high-flying clients, and his manner of speech, tailored to match. This chameleon quality is the one which makes him so very successful – not many others in smuggling circles can do this. Those who can are generally the leaders.

'Hardly! Why do you ask?'

The officer indicates a list displayed on the courthouse wall. 'There's money to be made these says. Big money. £500 if you can identify any of these men – known smugglers all.'

'What nonsense is this?' George looks at the list, the name Black Diamond right at the top, citing Seaford as the place where he is most likely to be found. No serious smuggler uses his own name; even without a £500 incentive it would make him far too easy to find. At least there's no mention of Crawford or Lewes.

Once over the surprise of finding his name displayed on the courthouse as a wanted man, he is astonished by the unfathomably huge sum of money now resting on his head.

'Do you know any of them?' The officer is hoping for some reflected glory. George shakes his head and turns abruptly away. He cannot stay here, and he has been struck completely dumb.

Disappointed, the officer heads back into the courthouse, unaware that he has so narrowly missed out on a great change in his own fortune.

George untethers his new roan from the trees, mounts, and heads south. He needs to call a council of war.

But first he has someone to see.

Chapter 33

Bishopstone, Sussex

Church of St Andrew

Jenny is picking spring flowers in the churchyard at Bishopstone. She and Richard have buried two of their three dead children here and she puts flowers on their grave every week. Mary Lucy, the third child, is in Seaford.

She has sent Dickon to forage for what food he can find, and James to fish at the creek. Ann plays happily by the gate to the park at Bishopstone Place and Elizabeth, barely walking, hangs off her skirt as usual.

She sits back, despairing, on the grass.

Where is Richard? She had wanted to believe him when he said he would not be gone long – that all would be sorted out in Horsham – but as the days have gone on, she is increasingly doubting his optimism.

It is so hard for her, alone. With Richard no longer fishing for the Duke or digging out the reservoir for the new tide mill there is no money coming in. She has four mouths to feed beside her own and it was never easy, even before her husband was taken. She is with child again. She needs to eat.

'Jenny.'

George – he must have brought Richard from Horsham! But Richard isn't with him. Perhaps he's at home already.

Hope fades as soon as she looks at him. He looks grimmer than she's ever seen him, and she can't decide what she feels about him. He is her husband's best friend and has supported them generously whenever he could.

There have been times when she has hated him, but this isn't one of them. If anyone can help them now it's George. She knows he would never willingly do them harm, but she also knows he is somehow at the bottom of all their current troubles. She and James have talked about this endlessly since Richard has been gone. Here he is now, come specially to find her. Why?

'George?'

'Jenny.' It's the only word he has. How does he tell her? Jenny and Richard should have been together for another twenty or thirty years. He knows no couple happier or more devoted. He knows no people better or more honest. The cruelty of it leaves him lost for words, but he must find some.

'Come into the church Jenny love. Come with me.' He can be kind and gentle when he must.

She stands reluctantly and he is shocked. There is nothing of her. Her belly, heavy with child, sticks out unnaturally from the skin and bones which carry it.

'Ann, play with Elizabeth while I go into the church with Uncle George.' The girl runs across and takes Elizabeth's hand. 'Come Lizzie – let's pick flowers for Jude and Jane – there are plenty over there.' She leads her away towards the bottom of the churchyard, sensing this is what her mother wants her to do.

George follows Jenny into the coolness of the church, past the big square font with its memories of happier days, up to the chancel where he sits her down in the priest's chair. He stands over her and draws breath, dreading what is to come.

'Where's Richard, George – is he with you – is he coming?'
She knows in her heart he is not. He would be here.

'He won't be coming Jenny – they have taken him to
London. I was in Horsham yesterday and saw him go.'

'London? Why?'

No other way but to tell her everything as fast as he can.

'He was found likely to be guilty of smuggling at the
hearing in Horsham and has been sent to London for trial.'

Just a delay then.

'But he's not a smuggler George – you know he's not. He'll
have to be released – how long do you think it will take?'

Her eyes. It's always her eyes. Still burning with hope,
looking to him to keep the flame alive.

'No Jenny. I don't think he'll be coming home.' Trying to
explain why seems pointless and telling her his own friendship
is at the root of all this is something he just can't face.

'The colonies – will they send him to the colonies? I don't
care where we are so long as we're together. We can go with
him.' The flame refuses to go out.

Finally. His choice. Tell her Richard will hang, which he
certainly will, or let her cling to false hope.

Hope seems the better course, at least until the child is
born. He must somehow find a way to get her through the birth
when she will be stronger. Her situation is desperate. The
efforts of the boys to feed them is falling a long way short and
she cannot work in this state. Better to wait until the trial is over
before crushing her hope irrevocably. She will be stronger once
the child is born.

'We must wait and see what happens, Jenny. Go home.
Build your strength – James and Dickon can find food for you.
Let me take Ann and Elizabeth home with me now to Dodo.
She will care for them until everything is clear.'

'No!' Losing their girls, even for a short while, is

unthinkable. What will Richard say if he comes back and finds them gone?

'Jenny. Please. Let me bring them to Dodo.'

'We could all come. You have plenty of room and Dodo won't mind.' She knows this is right because Dodo has often said so. She has resisted the notion up till now, but suddenly the solidity of the Lewes house and a plentiful supply of food has its appeal.

Agony upon agony. He cannot take her to Lewes without risking her life which could be forfeit if she's found in his company. Turning her down in her despair is cruel but there is no alternative, and he has already been here too long.

'No Jenny, I can't. You must at home with James and Dickon in case Richard comes back and doesn't know where you are.' He hates himself. 'The boys can look after you, but they can't look after the girls. Come, I must go.'

'Please George – help me! Don't leave us here without the girls.' If she did but know it, he's helping in the only way he can. He cannot wait, now, to get away.

'No Jenny. It's the right thing to do. Stay here and wait for Richard. I will bring the girls back when he comes.' It must be done.

Out in the pale sunshine they walk to the girls. Daffodils are bright on the tiny mound.

'Would you like a ride on my horse Ann – Elizabeth? Your Aunt Dodo would like to see you and I promised I would bring you to her when I left.'

Ann looks to Jenny, excited at the prospect of adventure but needing her mother's approval.

What mother does not put on the bravest face she can for her children? It breaks her heart.

'Come girls!' It's the work of a moment to lift them up, then mount and turn away towards Lewes.

132

'I've men out waiting for news. I'll bring it as soon as I have it.'

Her hope turns to despair. Her eyes are wet with tears; the flame is finally extinguished.

Chapter 34

Newgate Prison, London
Main Gate

Dick Whittington looks down implacably as Richard's cart trundles through the Newgate Prison entrance and stops at the lodge. Richard, never having heard of his namesake, does not notice.

'Name?'

'Ashcroft, sir. Richard Ashcroft.'

'Put out your arm, Ashcroft.' The command is one not to be questioned.

Attaching the heavy iron shackle is the work of a moment, and shortly there is one on his leg too. He is the only one in his batch of inmates to receive this attention. The authorities must consider his crime serious enough to warrant permanent fettering in case of attempted escape but this nuance is lost on Richard.

'Put him in the hold.' He is taken roughly by the arm and forced through a hatch into the room which lies between the top and bottom of a nearby arch. What seems at first to be pitch darkness slowly lifts a little.

He is in a room about twenty feet in length and fifteen in

breadth with a floor of stone. He gradually makes out a mass of bodies on a raised wooden barrack bed. The stench is overwhelming.

'Your arm again, Ashcroft, if you please.' He complies and the iron on his arm is attached to a ring bolt above the sleeping-bench, severely limiting his choice of places to try and find rest. One tiny window is trying its best to shed light on the appalling scene to little effect.

Richard has no idea how he comes to be here. He has been traveling all day on the cart with very little to eat or drink as he has been transferred for trial from Horsham to Newgate. It is all beyond him. There has been a terrible mistake and he still thinks someone must soon come to take him out of this dreadful place – take him back to his family, his fishing and the creek. Hope has not yet completely deserted him.

He dozes, exhausted, unable to lie down because of the fetters, slumped on the bit of bench he has managed to force his way onto. He soiled himself long ago and is ashamed. If he thought about it, his nose would tell him he is not alone in this.

'Ashcroft!' Over him looms the warder who brought him here. Time has no meaning. He could have been here two hours or two days – he's beyond knowing.

'Two and sixpence will do it!'

Richard peers through the gloom, wondering what this could possibly mean.

'Come, man. Give me two and sixpence and I will take you out of here to the common side.'

Richard cannot remember the last time he had as much as two and sixpence if he ever did. His life is measured in pennies and whatever he can scavenge from land and sea. He may as well have been asked for the moon.

'I have no money, sir. I have nothing to give.'

'A shilling then, to stay here.'

He really does not have any money. Even if he had he would not pay it to stay in this abominable place. His brain, never quick, does not grasp that the alternative must be far worse.

'I'm sorry sir. I have no money.'

'Not even a shilling? Six pence?' The warder does this every day and knows who is worth the squeeze and who has no chance of paying him anything. There are few prisoners who touch him; Richard's politeness and respect has already made him one of these but there's nothing for it but to move him.

Not roughly, but firmly then, Richard is uncoupled from the bolt in the wall and taken out through the hatch, barely able to stand.

There is a water trough at hand and the warder pushes him towards it to drink, which he does, greedily. The water is foul but quenches his raging thirst and for this he is pathetically grateful.

They pass through a door which bears the legend 'Middle Ward', but Richard cannot read. It is lighter than the place he has come from but there's no other real improvement. Steps lead from its centre and Richard is pushed down them. The warder does not follow him. A trapdoor bangs shut. It is completely dark.

Beyond despair now, Richard pulls himself up to sit, sensing bodies around him, how many he cannot tell.

'Where am I? Jenny, where am I?' He cries out to the love of his life, but he knows no answer can come from her. She does not have any idea where he is and for that, at least, he is grateful.

'You're in the stone hold my friend.' The voice is rough and close by. 'Welcome to hell.'

'Why am I here? What is this place?'

'It's where they put us as has no means to buy our way out

to somewhere better. Are you due for trial or have you already been condemned to serve time?'

'I think I must go for trial sometime soon, but I do not know when or understand why.' In truth, he knows absolutely nothing about anything happening to him.

'For your own sake, get rid of your clothes if you still have them, man. They are no good to you and will harbour pestilence – we are all as naked here as God made us. There is no other way which will not make you sick.'

'Take off my clothes and lie here naked?' Richard is appalled by the suggestion. His companion shrugs in the dark and smiles to himself. One night in here with the rats chewing at his breeches will change his mind. Everyone learns with enough time.

Richard weeps, finally. Silently at first but the misery wells up from the depths and he gulps the fetid air between sobs as the horror of it washes over him.

'That'll do you no good – shut up. No-one cares.' From all around come curses and threats to do him who knows what harm if he does not stay quiet and let these poor wretches sleep. It's all they have left to do.

Suddenly there is light from the hatch above. A bucket is lowered, and bread thrown down into the stinking liquid on the pavement floor. There is a rush of naked men to grab food and gulp water while they can. Richard is hungry and thirsty but still not inured enough to his conditions to stop himself being horrified when he finds he is surrounded by naked strangers. He gets a little bread but does not try to drink. He had almost enough at the trough on the way here.

To a man, his companions fall away from the light to whatever space they can find. The door slams shut.

He is utterly desolate and very afraid.

Chapter 35

Lewes, Sussex

George Crawford's House

'There must be something more you can do.' Dorothy Crawford and her husband are at breakfast, places for Ann and Elizabeth now empty after they have got down from table to play. She has willingly accepted the two girls into the house and into her heart. She and George have no children of their own and these two happy creatures have gone some way to filling the void.

'Anything I do will only make things worse, wife. I could visit him in Newgate. I could send in money to ease his conditions. I could testify at his trial. I could bring Jenny and the boys here to join Ann and Elizabeth but any of those things coming from me would put them in mortal danger as you well know.'

She does. She knows the new law could extract the ultimate sacrifice from anyone staying with him, but nobody yet knows how it will be applied. Being in the company of a smuggler as his wife or friend, as opposed to being in the company of a smuggler going about his business are two different things. She is hoping they will make the distinction, especially in her case.

She always knew him for what he was. She loves him for who he is, though she is aware that there are dark things about him she will never know. He has not risen to where he is through kindness and compassion, but she never confronts this, preferring only to see the George who is loyal to a fault and generous to his friends. She has been happy to enjoy the rewards from his way of life and has steeled herself against the time when he will no longer be with her.

Both she and George are deeply unsettled by what is happening to Richard and the way it has come about. She has not been able to see Jenny – her husband has decreed that they must stay completely away from Bishopstone if Richard is to have any chance of being declared an innocent man. Dorothy understands the logic of this but doing nothing is hard.

'Surely someone will speak for him? Are we all to sit by and let him hang without making any attempt to make them see they've got completely the wrong man? How will we live with ourselves?'

His wife's questions go over the same old ground. He has left no stone unturned, trying to find men willing to go to London to testify to Richard's innocence or give him character references at his trial. He has been willing to pay expenses for anyone who will come forward, has even tried threat and blackmail, all to no avail. The crown has done its work well. Everyone is too afraid. No-one will help.

He should do it himself, of course. He could tell exactly what happened on the day of the raid, how Richard had been there to help him only by chance, not as a member of his gang. He could tell how often he has tried to persuade his friend to be exactly what they are accusing him of being, but that he has always failed in the attempt.

He could do all these things, but he knows it would make

no difference and he's certain it would cost him his own life to try.

No. The best he can do now is go to London until it's all over and watch and wait for any chance to get Richard out of there. He'll stay at the Nag's Head till it's done.

But he won't go alone.

Chapter 36

Newgate Prison, London
June 4th, Early Morning

'Ashcroft, get up here!' The hatch is thrown open and far above him Richard can see the warder peering into the depths of the common hold.

'Here you go! Now you'll see – don't think you'll be coming back here again!' The men around him know why he's been called – where he's going – but Richard is still innocent enough to wonder if this means he's being set free. If these awful men are not expecting to see him again, he must be going home surely?

Covering himself as best he can he climbs the stone steps naked and ashamed, and wonders who will meet him at the gate. He hopes it's George, not Jenny. He does not want her to see him like this.

'Follow me.' The warder heads back towards the lodge, retracing the path they had taken when he first arrived.

'What's happening? Am I free? How will I get home?' There is no answer – his gaoler is not cruel enough to tell him.

The water when it hits him is cold, so cold.

'Wash yourself down man and put this on.' A coarse grey

tunic is thrust at him, not much better than rags, but at least he will be decent when he gets outside. He rubs himself down, looking expectantly at the warder for a second bucketful to rinse off the muck he has dislodged as best he can. It comes, and after he has washed, he pulls on the tunic feeling happy. He doesn't know how, but at last his ordeal is over; he will see Jenny again soon.

'This way.'

But now things take an unexpected turn. Remembering how he came in, he looks left to the main gate, which remains firmly shut. Perhaps people leave this awful place a different way. The warder produces a hefty key and unlocks a door straight ahead which Richard did not notice before.

'Through here.'

They're in a tunnel, not deep – he can see daylight through the windows up near the roof – but too long for him to be able to see to the end. There is a sharp turn right which brings him to a flight of steps.

'Up you go.'

'But where does it lead? Who is up there?'

The warder has had pity for this man from the day he came in, never more so than now, but he cannot help.

'Just go up Richard – I will be here when you come down.'

He climbs. There are people up there – a lot of people, all talking. The noise is harsh to ears used to near-silence and continues to grow as he climbs. Suddenly it stops; it stops as he enters the dock; as the people in the courtroom see him for the first time; as he finally grasps where he is.

The disappointment is crushing. He sinks onto the bench, hugging himself, and stares at the ground, utterly betrayed. Nearby there is a man wearing a wig who will make some pretense of defending him, but even he knows there is only one way this will end.

Chapter 37

Sessions House, Old Bailey, London
June 4th, Morning

Sir Dudley Ryder, Attorney General, gets to his feet and opens the case against Richard, having discussed it at length with his friend Newcastle over dinner the previous evening.

Newcastle had been very pleased with himself when talking about the new Parliamentary Act the night before. Both he and Ryder know there is only one outcome for this trial when Richard is found guilty – which he will be. No room for manoeuvre at all.

Ryder is also buoyed by the knowledge that every customs man to be called to give evidence works for Newcastle. Their testimony is not in doubt. This will be an easy win.

Sir Dudley gets to his feet and addresses the court. He begins by helpfully explaining the recent change in the law and the reasons for it:

'May it please your lordship, and you gentlemen of the jury, the prisoner at the bar stands indicted for a crime of a very high

nature, under the terms of a recent Act of Parliament, passed for the preservation of the constitution, and the general peace of the kingdom.

'The Act was made in the last session of Parliament in order to prevent malefactors running goods and going armed in great numbers to the terror of many of the inhabitants of the country.

'To put a stop to that practice, the legislature thought it proper to make the law I am now to state to you.

'Gentlemen, the law now says that if any persons to the number of three or more, armed with fire arms, shall, after the 17th of July, 1746, attempt the carrying away, or landing of untaxed goods, or if they obstruct officers forcibly in the execution of their office, persons guilty of this offence, I am stating to you, they are made guilty without benefit of clergy.'

There it is then. Newcastle's shiny new law. Richard tries to listen to Sir Dudley but cannot grasp what he is saying. He still cannot see how being in South Lane at the time of the raid was a crime. Nor does he understand 'without benefit of clergy', which means 'with no possible appeal'.

Sir Dudley is only just getting into his stride. On he goes:

'Richard Ashcroft is charged with:

'unlawfully and feloniously, together with thirty other unknown persons, assembling, and gathering at Eastbourne in Sussex, on the 14th of September last;

'being armed with firearms, and other offensive weapons, in order to be aiding and assisting in the running and carrying away of untaxed goods, and goods liable to pay duties, which have never been paid or secured;

'and of unlawfully, riotously, raucously and feloniously

146

obstructing, opposing, and resisting the several officers who will appear before you in the due execution of their duties.'

These three charges are barely understood by Richard, alone in the dock. He knows he wasn't part of the gang, he knows he wasn't armed and he knows he had no confrontation with any of the officers.

He knows this to be true and fully expects it somehow to become clear to everyone very soon. It cannot be otherwise.

'The case of the prisoner stands thus:

'Upon the 14th of September last, Thomas Mortimer, and several riding officers of the customs stationed at Eastbourne, were at a place called Southland, where they came to intercept a gang of smugglers.

'Accordingly, about three o'clock in the afternoon, on the 14th of September, thirty or forty of these smugglers, several of whom were armed with fire arms, with about fifty or sixty horses, presented themselves to the officers of the customs.

'The officers asked them, what their horses were loaded with? They told them, by virtue of their office, they were bound to examine them.

'These persons made use of a great many oaths to terrify the officers of the customs; they presented their fire-arms, and swore they would blow their brains out if they attempted to seize their goods.

'Notwithstanding this the officers were not intimidated, but determined to secure the brandy and tea; accordingly they rode up and cut off several half anchors of brandy, and several bags of tea.

'Upon that the smugglers presented their pieces, swore they

would shoot them, drove away their horses, by which the officers were rendered incapable of seizing the goods.'

Richard, paying close attention now, recognises this as an accurate description of what he himself had witnessed at the bottom of South Lane. He is astonished, however, by what comes next:

'Gentlemen, the prisoner at the bar was one of this gang, and he had loaded upon the horse, on which he rode, four half anchors of brandy.

'Joseph Simpson, one of the officers of the customs, endeavoured to seize the brandy that was upon the prisoner's horse, but was prevented from doing it by the prisoner, who slipped the bridle or halter off the horse's head and drove the horse away.

'When Joseph Simpson pulled him off his horse, he swore, if he could get one of the company's pieces, he would shoot him through the head; he hollowed after the rest of the company to come to his assistance; but they were too careful of their goods to come back.'

It wasn't his horse, he doesn't have one. Everybody knows it. It was George's horse and he was never on it. Are these people stupid? He could only have removed the halter if he had been on the ground, not mounted. Richard needs this gentleman to see that although he was there he was not part of the gang. No-one, not Joseph Simpson or anyone else had ever pulled him off the horse. Dandy belongs to George Crawford and will not tolerate anyone else on his back.

But Sir Dudley is just getting started.

'One Mr Thomas Fletcher likewise saw the whole transaction, and particularly what passed with the prisoner at the bar. The other officers were likewise concerned in the same matter, and they will give you an account of the transaction I have mentioned.

'The Prisoner at this time got away but was afterwards seized and carried before his majesty's justices of the peace; and upon hearing what was alleged against him, he was committed to prison, and now stands indicted before you.'

The Attorney General has outlined the case accurately but added one detail. He has said Richard threatened to shoot Joseph Simpson.

Richard, stung by this, got to his feet and appealed to anyone who might listen: 'Sir, I was not armed. I could not have done what you are saying.' Unsurprisingly, no-one paid any heed.

No-one interrupts Sir Dudley in full flow. He knows his only job is to secure a guilty verdict. He's not too concerned with the rights or wrongs of this particular case.

'It is very important to us all that if he is guilty, he should be found so.'

'The practice of smuggling is grown so great that people know not how to lie safe in their beds for fear of them. Gentlemen, if it is proved that this man is a smuggler, I don't doubt but you will find him guilty.'

. . .

Sir Dudley doesn't doubt it and nor does anyone else.

Except Richard.

Chapter 38

Sessions House, Old Bailey, London
June 4th, Afternoon

Richard sits in the dock watching the great man, dumbfounded. He has no idea what Ryder is talking about. He has been in court while it has been explained but he is in no state to have taken it in. He still believes he will be found innocent – you can't be in much trouble for helping a friend surely? Ryder begins his case.

'Call Joseph Simpson.'

Simpson, the arresting officer, who is the last person to have seen Richard with Jenny, takes the stand.

'Do you know the prisoner at the bar?'
  'Yes, sir, I saw him the 14th of September last with a gang of smugglers.'

. . .

Simpson is very eager to please.

'How many smugglers might there be?'
  'Thirty and upwards.'

Simpson remembers it well. Another occasion where being outnumbered left them empty handed.

'Give an account of how they were going, and what they were carrying?'
  'They were carrying brandy and tea upon horses' backs, slung with cords.'
  'How were they prepared for defence?'
  'There were three that had arms, and they presented their arms several times; one was a blunderbuss, and the other two guns, and they had whips and sticks.'
  'Give an account what they did to you; where was this?'
  'In South Lane. We went to attack them.'
  'Were they under any command?'

Simpson cannot answer this accurately. He couldn't have seen George Crawford – he had run for cover right at the start.

'They drew themselves up together sir, and their lead horses were in the middle.'

. . .

He manages to skirt round the question and come up with an inadequate answer. Ryder is disappointed but presses on.

'You went up and demanded the goods of them?'
   'Yes, because they were running of it, and we thought it our duty to seize it; they swore we should not have any of it.'

Bitterness creeps into his voice at this. He well remembers them getting away.

   Ryder presses his man:

'What followed upon that?'
   'They threatened to fire, and their three pieces were presented to us several times.'
   'Was any discharged?'
   'No, none discharged.'

Which isn't quite true. Shots were fired over the heads of his men, but Simpson has no wish to let it be thought he was threatened or frightened in any way.

   Ryder turns and looks at Richard.

'What about this man?'
   'I pulled him off his horse.'

At this, Richard sits forward. He was never on a horse. It was George's and he was left holding it.

. . .

'What had he upon his horse?'
  'Four half anchors.'
  Simpson is warming to his task now.
  'Did he resist you?'

Ryder turns to look at Richard again and waits for what he knows is coming from the customs man.

'He swore he would shoot me as soon as I pulled him off; he then pull'd the bridle or halter off the horse's head, and the horse ran away.'

Richard starts to stand; he knows this can't be right and thinks perhaps Simpson is confused. He was never on the horse; he couldn't have been pulled off it and he has never held a firearm in his life.

'Did you hold him?'
  'No, he got off.'

Again untrue.

'Did you seize any of the goods?'
  'Yes, thirty half anchors of brandy, and half a bag of tea.'
      . . .

Now the fear starts. This is so far from the truth that Richard is stunned. The customs men got nothing. The horses were sent away carrying the cargo. Only the bags of tea on George's horse and the brandy with it were ever anywhere near the officers.

'Can you be sure it is the same man; did you ever see him before?'
    'I have seen him a great many times.'
    'What business did he follow?'
    'He used to be a day-labouring man till he took to the trade of smuggling.'

'Not so – it's not right – I was never a smuggler in my life!' Richard casts round for someone to help him, someone to make this stop.

'Was the prisoner one of those that were drawn up in the manner you described just now?'
    Ryder ploughs on regardless.
    'He was among them, yes sir.'

'I was there, yes, but –'
    Richard's council finally intervenes;

'Had the prisoner any arms?'

. . .

Richard has told him exactly what happened and he is inclined to believe his client was unarmed. Simpson must be careful here.

'I did not see anything...'

This answer is not helpful. Ryder has already told the court he was armed and that Simpson and the others would say so. He tries a different tack.

'You have known him a good many years. I'll venture to ask you, what has been his general character?'
'A very bad one of late; he had the character that he used to smuggle, but I never saw him with any goods.'

This last admitted with reluctance.
Richard gets to his feet:

'Did not you declare before the Justice of the Peace in Horsham, that I had not any firearms, or anything to molest them with?'

Simpson knows this is exactly what he said to the magistrates. It will be on record in Horsham. He is forced to tell the truth about the pistol.

. . .

'He had no firearms as I know of...'

Richard sits down and looks around him at this – the officer has confirmed that he had no pistol. What Mr Ryder said is not true.

'... but he swore he would shoot me, if he could get one of the pieces that the company had.'

Simpson does his best to retrieve things. Not having a gun but threatening to use one if he had one is the best he can do here.

Ryder moves swiftly on:

'How came you to let him get away?'
    'He went away on foot. We went after the gang.'
    'Did you get all the brandy and tea?'
    'We did not get near all, they carried it off.'

He has already said they got it all. Again, Ryder steps in quickly.

'Did he go off with the gang?'

Simpson thinks hard. He looks at Richard and perhaps feels pity?

.   .   .

157

'I can't say that.'

No. He can't. He knows he didn't.

Chapter 39

Sessions House, Old Bailey, London
4th June, Afternoon

'*Call Thomas Fletcher.*'

Ryder hopes Fletcher is less squeamish than Simpson seems to have been.

'*What is your business?*'
    '*I am a riding officer in East Dean.*'
    '*How long have you known the prisoner?*'
    '*I have known him seven years.*'
    '*Give an account of what you know in relation to the prisoner?*'
    '*We met a company of about thirty. When they saw us come up, they drew up in a body; we went up and asked them for their goods, and said we were custom house officers. They said we should have nothing; we said we would have all, and I saw Simpson pull the prisoner off his horse.*'

. . .

Richard's head sinks into his hands. He was never on the horse – why would they say this?

'*Did you take away any tea and brandy?*'
    '*We seized 30 half anchors of brandy, and one bag of tea; we cut them off from the horses.*'

Only the goods on George's horse were cut free, the rest were driven away with the horses to keep it from the customs men.

'*When you asked for these goods what answer did they make?*'
    '*They swore we should not have any of them. They called for the persons to come up with firearms, and they presented their firearms at us five.*'

He is warming to his task now.

'*We told them that they might fire if they would.*'

A preposterous thing to say but no-one challenges it.

'*With that we rode up to them directly, and cut it off their horses, and some went one way and some another; some they carried off.*'
    '*Did you not see the prisoner at the bar among them? Did you see any struggle between the prisoner and Mr Simpson?*'

'I saw Simpson pull the prisoner off his horse.'

George's horse. George's horse. He was only holding it. Richard wants to scream it at him. This is just not right. Surely everyone knows he's never had his own horse in Bishopstone?

'What then?'
    'Then he ran away to the other side of the horse; and I heard him say, if he could get one of the pieces, he would shoot him.'

The light is dawning on Richard. He's a very simple man but he knows theatre when he sees it, though he may not know what to call it. These people have all learned their lines and rehearsed them well together.

'Did he call out to the company?'
    'Yes, at first he did.'
    'Did you observe whether he pulled the bridle off the horse?'
    'I did not see him.'

Ironic, because Richard knows he pulled the bridle off the horse, but to describe that accurately Fletcher would have to admit he was on the ground – he couldn't have been on the horse.

'When this fray was over between Simpson and him, what became of the company?'

'We pursued them about half a mile, and we then carried off what we could.'

Richard's council rises again.

'I am instructed to ask this question; What is the man's general character?'

Fletcher thinks about this; like Simpson had before him. He does not look at Richard.

'I can't say a great deal of his character, he has not the character for stealing anything, but he has been of late a little troublesome.'

Ryder needs more than this.

'Is it his general character that of being a smuggler?' He prompts.
    'Yes, he has the character for it.'

Which is not the same as saying he actually is one, but it's the best Ryder is going to get.

Chapter 40

Sessions House Old Bailey, London
4th June, Afternoon

Ryder takes stock. Three witnesses must be enough, surely?'

'Call Thomas Mortimer.'

'Mr Mortimer – what are you?'

'I am a riding officer at Eastbourne. On the 14th of September last, I saw a great company of people in the South Lane.'

'Who was with you?'

'Mr Smith, Mr Hurst, Mr Fletcher, and Mr Simpson.'

'What had they with them?'

'Brandy and tea, loaded upon horses. When we came up to them, they drew up in a body together, and we asked them what they had. We said we would have it all; then they presented their firearms, two or three long pieces.'

This, at least, is accurate, but none was presented by Richard.

• • •

'One was a brass piece; they presented these pieces and swore we should have none of the goods. One of them, when I came up first, struck me across the head.'

'Did any other strike you?'

Ryder is expectant here. He waits for his answer.

'No, I don't know the prisoner.'

This is not an answer to the question Ryder asked him. Ryder knows right away this is not at all helpful. It indicates Mortimer knows he is supposed to be testifying against Richard, and he is expected to confirm everything already said.

A key witness blurting out, under pressure, that he does not recognise or know the prisoner is the worst possible thing to happen. Ryder sits down.

All three of Newcastle's men were called to say they knew the prisoner and condemn him. None did a really good job and as for Mortimer, he would never have called him if he'd known he would admit he had no idea who Richard was.

But still. Ryder decides to cut his losses. He dares not risk calling the other two revenue men. He's already called one more than he said he would and it hasn't worked out well.

Chapter 41

Sessions House, Old Bailey, London
4th June, Afternoon

'Call the prisoner to the bar.'

'What have you to say in your defence?'

The judge looks at the wretch in front of him. He appears to be the only person in court who has no idea what is happening here.

Richard looks at the court. Looks at the great men around him. Nothing in his simple life has prepared him for this.

'Please ye, my Lord, as I was going along the road I met these people accidentally, but what Mr Simpson says of my saying I would fire at him, is entirely false.'

. . .

Something about the quietness of the man brings the court to a hush. The men normally tried here are of a different cut – harsher, angrier – easier to judge.

'I have a wife and eight children, and had it not been in the daytime, I should have had no business there, and I had no arms nor nothing for defence; I had nothing in my hand to obstruct the officers or defend myself, and I never followed the affair.'

He is whispering the truth and all hear it. All but Richard know it has no relevance to the business at hand.

'Please ye, my Lord, I could have had thirty people to my character, but I have not the wherewithal to do it, for I have nothing to support myself.'

Looking at him in the dock in his borrowed, tattered filth, none doubts that.

They are here to convict him of being a violent criminal – worse – by implication, the leader of hundreds of violent criminals. Such a man would surely not look like this.

Richard has nothing more to say. He sits again, head in hand.

His council gets to his feet.

'I have one more witness to call.'

. . .

Richard lifts his head. George. It must be George, come to tell them this is all a dreadful mistake. Surely his friend is come to do this, even at great personal cost?

But it is not George.

'What is your name sir?'
'James Ashcroft.'

Richard looks at his son, seventeen years old, grown so tall, standing straight, come to speak for his father. He can hardly contain his gratitude and pride.

'What relation are you to the prisoner?'
'He is my own father.'
'What business does your father follow?'
'He never follows any other business than fishing and working under my lord Duke; he works under my lord Duke a-fishing, under the Duke of Newcastle, he has worked under him a great many years farming and fishing. I never knew him guilty of smuggling.'

The boy is not cowed. He is telling the truth. He loves his father and knows him to be nothing but good.

'Is he a man in good circumstances?'

James shrugs at this.

. . .

'He is in no circumstances to bear the expense of witnesses coming to town.'

At that, James sits down, what little he has had to contribute over and done.

Again, the judge turns to Richard.

'Prisoner have you anything else to say?'

Richard, finally overcome by the enormity of it all, has nothing left.

'I can say nothing for myself, but that I happened to be there accidentally; and I could have had many to have appeared for me, could I have borne the expense of it.'

He sinks back onto the bench and drops his head into his hands. He does not see the jury huddle. Does not know they have nothing to consider. Does not know that for the last two months just being there with George was enough.

Chapter 42

Sessions House, Old Bailey, London
4th June, Afternoon

'Have you reached a verdict on which you are all agreed?'

The foreman of the jury makes the most of his moment and takes his time.

'Yes, my Lord. We find the prisoner guilty as charged.'

A general stirring goes round the court. This is the bit they all came for.

Richard lifts his head and sees that from somewhere a black square has appeared on the judge's head. What can this mean? Everything is beyond him and has been ever since he left Bishopstone.

'Prisoner at the bar you have been found guilty of smuggling. You are a threat to all peace-loving people. Under the terms of the new Smuggling Act I have no other penalty open to me. You will be taken from here to the tree at Tyburn, there to be hung by the neck until you are dead.'

· · ·

Hung? For what? He carried a barrel and held a horse. He cannot make any sense of it. But this isn't the end of it. The judge, like Ryder before him, is getting into his stride.

'After you are dead you will be cut down from the tree, taken to Shepherd's Bush and gibbeted there on the road for all to see what befalls anyone engaging in smuggling in this year of our Lord 1747.'

The hush is deadly. This is more than anyone, except Ryder and the judge, had expected.

'Please sir, for the love of God, have mercy!'

Richard finds voice from somewhere.

'I have a poor sick wife at home and eight children. Do not take me from them — we have never done harm to anyone. I helped my friend — you cannot kill me for that — it is every man's Christian duty.'

Poor Richard. The number of children is wrong; the eighth is not yet born and three are dead; and no-one knows where his wife is.

. . .

'Sentence has been passed. I cannot change it now. You have permission to appeal to the King.'

Poor Richard again. The King approved the Act which makes this sentence irreversible.

Richard was there in South Lane. He has said so. Which is what signed his death warrant.

He never had a chance.

Chapter 43

Ordinary of Newgate's House, London

4th June, Evening

John Taylor, Ordinary of Newgate has seen many condemned men. As the spiritual advisor at Newgate, he has spent time with some of the most notorious and ugly villains at their lowest points. He sees them when they return to Newgate after trial, he ministers to them at a special service on the night before they die, and he travels with them to the tree in Tyburn lest they should want to make confession at the last moment.

He is also able to top up his miserable stipend by writing and selling accounts of his meetings with them to the general populace which does not seem to be able to get enough of them.

There are eight hanging sessions each year with at least five men hung each time. His eighty accounts a year (two for each prisoner) sell for sixpence each, and he produces at least a thousand of each.

The house he now sits in is, therefore, a very comfortable one. He has just returned from his first meeting with Richard Ashcroft, condemned to death at the Old Bailey today for smuggling.

He is troubled by the man whose gentleness and heartfelt

belief that somehow it will be proved he has done nothing wrong has touched him. Richard's bewilderment feels genuine, his despair only too real.

Richard, still wearing the rough tunic given him to cover himself up for his trial, had fallen on the Ordinary with a passion – anxious to know if he can help him escape his fate, if he can find news of his wife, if he can get messages to her from this dreadful place.

Much as the Ordinary would like to help, he has seen enough to know the case is hopeless and Richard will certainly die. He is used to meeting men facing death. Some are angry, some frightened, some loudly protest their innocence. Very few are bewildered. They are usually hardened criminals who know precisely how the law works, how they have broken it and why they must pay the price.

Richard appears to know none of these things. He seemed not to understand what is happening to him, how dire his situation, when they spoke together earlier. His thoughts were focused entirely on his wife and children.

The Ordinary is in no position to head off for Sussex to try and find Jenny Ashcroft and bring her to Newgate to comfort her husband.

He can, though, use his network of priestly contacts to try and find news of her and he decides he will do this. It may bring a crumb of comfort to the wretched man.

Thus decided, he picks up his pen and composes his pamphlet.

'Richard Ashcroft, aged about 44 Years, was born at Lewes in Sussex. From his infancy he was bred to follow the plough, and other parts of husbandry, as his father had done before him, so that his education you may imagine was not much. At length he took to the trade of fishing for some years past, he says, at Bishopstone, in the said county, where he lived ever since he was married and left his father.

'His neighbours have given him the character of a quiet, harmless man till (unhappily for him) he was met in South Lane, and known by a dissolute and notorious gang of smugglers, who are become the terror of many of the inhabitants of the country.

'His being seen with people armed contrary to the recent Act of Parliament, (though he carried no manner of offensive weapon himself) was plainly proved against him at his trial; of which he confesseth himself very sensible, and much laments the unlucky and fatal day, not only that he was seen, but that he should ever be in such company. He persists in it to the uttermost that he never had any interest, or advantage among the smugglers.

'But as his employment of fishing led him down to the seaside, he was often in their company and drank with them, but protests, that by this means, and this alone it came to pass, that he was ever among them, at the time of his being with them, when sworn against, for which he suffers.

'While he was watching, a gang of smugglers had landed prohibited goods, and as he was going home, he met them conveying them away upon horses when the officers met the company with their cargo in South Lane. He knew —indeed, he owns – that they were about illicit business, but had not the least notion of an act, or proclamation, which might touch or affect him for being in such company. However, the sentence upon the fact proved against him, of being in company with three or more, who carried arms, contrary to express law, he confesses to be just, and gives himself up to this fate with all the patience and resignation which a man of his mean apprehension, and in such circumstances, may be supposed to be master of.

'He says further that reason sufficient he has to be grieved, and heartily to lament the evil ways of his past life, such as *profane cursing and swearing, and not keeping the sabbath according to the commandment. For which, and all offences of his life, he is in all appearance sincere in his repentance, rejoices to rely on the merits of our Saviour Jesus Christ for remission and salvation, and leaves this world in charity with all men.'*

This last paragraph is standard fare. He adds it to all his pamphlets, it being his job to save people's souls; no easier way to show he's doing it consistently well than to have them repent every time.

The rest is an accurate re-telling of Richard's miserable tale, as told to him in the prison chapel this afternoon. The unfortunate wretch has fallen foul of the new smuggling law but there's little doubt Richard had no idea it had been passed or what it meant.

Taylor sighs and puts down his pen. His job is to minister to the prisoner, not to think deeply about what is happening to him. But he will try and get news of Jenny. It's the least he can do for someone he thinks is, in all probability, a good and innocent man.

Chapter 44

Sussex Downs

The Road to Seaford Head

Jenny is bereft without the girls. They were young enough to keep her busy and busy is what she needed to be. Without them she has sunk into despair.

The boys spend their days looking for food and bring home what they find each evening. James is turning into a decent fisherman so there is usually at least one good-sized fish in the haul. She worries, though, that he does not have permission to do this on Newcastle's land. The consequences for all of them will be severe if he's caught poaching.

It does not occur to her, but a lot of blind eyes are being turned around her these days. There is an invisible shield round Richard's family; he's a decent man in trouble and everyone knows it. Jenny is loved for her dogged determination to keep going and has always been popular in the village.

But news of the new law has reached Bishopstone, and people are afraid to help openly. Turning a blind eye is all they can do. They all know Richard will not be coming home, but do not tell her or the boys. Nor will he be going to the colonies.

The time is fast approaching when she must be told, but no-one wants the job.

No-one needs to tell her, though. She has known since George took Ann and Elizabeth that he would only do such a thing if he knew Richard was not coming back. She also knows because nobody comes near.

She has spent the day walking. She set out early, straight after the boys had left, a hug for each of them as they went off towards the creek. Her destination lay the other way and her feet had taken her there without thought.

She and Richard have come this way so often. Their favourite place. Seaford Head, high above the sea which glitters far below between the head and the bright white of the Seven Sisters in the distance. The sisters soar over Cuckmere Haven – more George's territory than theirs. No, Seaford Head is their place. They courted there and have often come back even since the move to Bishopstone.

She sits near the cliff edge, still thinking. No picnic today. There have been so many here.

Richard. Where is he? She knows there is nothing worse they can do to him than keep him from her and their family. Nothing worse they can do to her than keep her from him. Why they are doing it she cannot tell. She stopped trying to fathom it long ago. She knows she will never see him again. Never know his fate.

She thinks of their children and the joy they brought. James, now a fine young man and Dickon not far behind, both ready to make their way into the world. Ann and Elizabeth are safe with Dodo, she is sure, but even Dodo and George are staying away from her now. She has not seen the girls since they left with George weeks ago. She hopes they remember her fondly.

Mary Lucy, golden child, lies safely in Seaford churchyard.

They never got to know Jude and Jane, who are not so far away, buried peacefully in the churchyard at Bishopstone.

The eighth child has died inside her she is sure. It has not moved for days. She has not told the boys – they would not grasp the significance. But she does. She knows she is not healthy enough to survive what lies ahead if she tries to deliver the dead child. If Richard were here, it would be different, she might try. But he's not.

Despairing, close to starving and exhausted, she calls to Richard one last time.

When did he ever let her down? He's there, of course, smiling, holding out his hand to support her.

She stands and takes it. He stays right there beside her as she walks forward and plunges into the sea far below.

Chapter 45

Kensington Palace, London

22nd July

George R

Newcastle is very pleased with the way things are going. He barely sees Richard as human; more a pawn in his everyday game of making money. He wastes no time thinking about the man, his wife or his family. One less peasant is one less mouth for the parish to feed. He hadn't been in court for the trial (better to lie low) so does not know that the man works for him and has never relied on the parish for anything.

He has come to Kensington Palace to make sure there is no last-minute hitch. Richard's appeal is in front of the King today.

'Remind me Newcastle. The new Smuggling Act – what exactly does it say?'

'Anyone caught in the act of smuggling, or in the company of smugglers while they are smuggling, must automatically be condemned to death, sire.'

'I thought so, but I am still not sure this law is just. I have before me here an appeal from a man who, by all accounts, has done little more than know some smugglers. For this I am asked to confirm that he must die.'

Occasionally the King really reads the papers put before

him. Newcastle sighs. This is not the case he would have chosen to be scrutinised. He decides to give him the full speech.

'Sire. The punishment of death is a necessity of society in certain stages of the civilising process. There are two great instincts which lie at the root of all penal law; without it the community neither feels it is sufficiently revenged on the criminal, nor thinks the example of his punishment is adequate to deter others from imitating him.'

'Meaning?' George hates flummery and is intensely irritated by the pomposity of this explanation.

'He has to die sire. When I first asked you to approve the amendment to the law I told you why we needed it. We need to make examples of these men to stop other people following them. This is the first example of a man convicted under the act.'

King George isn't going to make it easy.

'But the act allows the law to kill people for being in the company of smugglers! From what you tell me, Thomas, it would be hard to live in Sussex and NOT be in the company of smugglers whether they are actually smuggling at the time or not. Why this man? Why is he the first you bring before me?'

'Because he has condemned himself out of his own mouth. He has admitted he was there. He has admitted there were smugglers there. He has admitted he knew them.'

'Oh, but really –'

'I'm afraid, sire, you have no choice. He must die. He is condemned out of his own mouth. He has admitted he was there. That's all the law requires for him to die.'

'Yes, yes, I know. But I had not anticipated it being used so bluntly. This man, according to the Ordinary, is very ordinary himself, certainly not a vicious gang leader nor, as far as anyone can tell, a smuggler of any kind.'

'The very fact that he is not a vicious gang leader, just someone who was there – which, by the way, I rather think is the case – will send the most powerful message to the people; smuggling and smugglers must be stopped.

'When word of this death gets round people will close their doors to them. No longer will they be local heroes. They will be shunned, and their business will cease. Besides which, you cannot grant the appeal, majesty. The Act is watertight.'

'There is no way round it in law?'

'None, sire.'

Reluctantly the King lifts his pen, dips it and signs.

No reprieve.

Chapter 46

The Ordinary of Newgate's House
27th July

The Ordinary ushers the messenger out and returns to his desk, subdued. The news he has just received is not what he was expecting. He had wanted to hear news of Richard's wife from Sussex and, at the very least, be able to tell him she was bearing up nobly and wished him well. But, instead, he now knows the poor woman is dead, found at the bottom of Seaford Head while Richard has been in the condemned cell.

His job is to offer Richard comfort in his final moments. This news will be too much for the poor man to bear. He knows from what little time he has spent with him that the man thinks nothing of himself but talks only of Jenny and his family; how they are faring and whether he will ever see them again. It's too awful.

Taylor does not want to think about it, so, finding the Ashcroft pamphlet adds the following:

'He had a wife and seven children when he was apprehended and brought to Newgate; but since his conviction his wife has

died and the seven poor helpless orphans are left without any other provision but what the laws of the land may oblige their native parish to make for their subsistence.'

His sources for this were inaccurate if he did but know it. In the years between their marriage and Richard's arrest three of their eight children (the prisoner had been right about the number), and one unborn, have died, leaving Ann and Elizabeth in the care of friends and James and Dickon facing the world on their own.

The Ordinary's next visit to Newgate was already going to be difficult. It came as no surprise that Richard's appeal had been turned down. The prisoner himself, when last he saw him, remained pathetically hopeful; the King would put things right. Now he must be told all is lost.

Nothing can stop the dreadful pantomime he must shortly witness.

Taylor knows his first job is to save Richard's soul. In his heart he believes him to be the victim of a cruel miscarriage of justice and therefore thinks this task is not necessary.

Secondly, he must minister to him right up to the end at Tyburn and ease his passing as best he can.

Richard cannot be shielded from the horror of his impending death, but he does not have to know his wife and unborn child are dead in such dreadful circumstances. Nor that two of his remaining children, James and Richard, are doing all they can to avoid being thrown into the poor house where they would rely solely on the goodness of their parish.

It would comfort him to know his two daughters are in safe keeping in Lewes but he cannot reveal this without telling everything else he has found out.

He sits for a long time in contemplation. Shadows lengthen and he must go. Richard is waiting to hear his fate.

He must die. That's enough, surely. Why burden him with the rest of it?

Chapter 47

Newgate Prison, London
28th July

'I'm sorry Richard, the King does not grant your appeal. You must die tomorrow.'

The Ordinary can hardly bear to look at the man as this news hits home. The piteousness of it makes his decision easy. He will not tell Richard that Jenny is dead.

'If the King thinks so, then so be it, though I still do not know why it must be. I will try to be brave sir, but it's hard.' He thinks a bit. 'Jenny. Will I see Jenny? Will she be there? It will be hard for her, but I should like to see her again and it would be a comfort if she was there at my end.'

The Ordinary cannot lie. Nor can he burst this bubble of hope with the truth. He decides to avoid the question altogether.

'I think, Richard, you should make your peace with God. Make confession and I will give you the sacrament.'

As if on cue, a bell begins to toll as they make their way to the chapel, Richard's irons clanking on the pavement as they go. It is the evening bell of St. Sepulchre's. Over a hundred years ago a benefactor had left an amount of fifty pounds in trust to the church to ensure its bell is tolled on the night before every execution in the city. It will also be tolling tomorrow morning, as Richard passes on his way to Tyburn.

He and the four men who are to die beside him can hear the dismal sound throughout the chapel service.

Richard makes his confession as best he can. Taylor grants him absolution, though in truth he cannot really see what for. The man has confessed nothing more than being in the wrong place at the wrong time and God needs no help from an Ordinary to take pity and forgive such a man. The service unfolds, the sacrament is administered and the Ordinary offers what he hopes is a helpful sermon.

Richard's eyes are drawn continuously to the black coffin beside the minister. Tomorrow, he supposes, he will be in a coffin himself and thinks, vaguely, that to be at rest in such a thing will at least be release from his living hell. The part of his sentence requiring him to be gibbeted at Shepherd's Bush went right over his head. There will be no peaceful rest for him. No coffin. Just a cage.

Now he is thrown into the condemned hold – unimaginably worse than anywhere he has been before. It's pitch dark, which is fortunate; only two of his senses – smell and touch – are assaulted by the open sewer running through its centre. From this hell-hole he can hear another bell. A hand-bell this time, in the prison yard. The crier cries as others have cried here before him from time immemorial, but Richard is beyond hearing or understanding it.

All you that in the condemned hole do lie,
Prepare you, for tomorrow you shall die;
Watch all and pray; the hour is drawing near,
That you before the Almighty must appear.

Examine well yourselves; in time repent,
That you may not to eternal flames be sent.
And when St. Sepulchre's Bell in the morning tolls,
The Lord above have mercy on your souls.'

Chapter 48

Newcastle House, London
28th July

Newcastle House is a handsome three-storey building in Lincoln's Inn Fields, roughly halfway between Newgate and Tyburn, so a convenient place for the great and the good to gather before heading out to the showcase hanging in the morning. A short carriage ride will take them there or, if the crowds are too thick, a thirty-minute walk will do it.

Newcastle's guests this evening include his brother, Henry Pelham the Prime Minister, Charles Lennox the Duke of Richmond, Dudley Ryder the Attorney General, and William Gorringe JP, the senior magistrate from Horsham. All these men have played an integral part in bringing about tomorrow's events. All of them fully understand what they have done in bringing Richard Ashcroft to die at Tyburn in the morning and why Newcastle has required them to do it. All are far too savvy to acknowledge that there is anything untoward about the proceedings they are in town to witness.

'The death of smuggling.' Lord Newcastle raises his glass expectantly and the toast is taken up by them all.

The toast should really be 'The death of smuggling in Sussex' which is what actually concerns the gentlemen gathered here. Newcastle owns 40,000 acres of prime East Sussex land which, despite the recent enclosures, he cannot exploit properly until there are no more gangs rampaging across them. Richmond owns 12,000 acres of West Sussex, at Goodwood.

First and foremost, both need the loyalty of everyone living on their land. Smugglers are still seen as heroes in the villages; harboured, aided and abetted and able to cheat the law with impunity. Newcastle and Richmond agreed long ago this could not continue.

Henry Pelham, Prime Minister by virtue of his brother's machinations on the departure of Walpole, steered the Act through Parliament, thus ensuring death for anyone proved to have been in the company of smugglers, which Richard Ashcroft was, by his own admission.

Sir Dudley Ryder and Mr Gorringe have played their legal parts. If either had doubts about the weakness of the case against Richard for smuggling, or the extreme harshness of the death penalty and gibbeting just for being there, neither chose to act on them.

'It looks as if we shall have a good day for it.' Sir Dudley looks out over Lincoln's Inn Fields, which bask in the evening sunlight.

'I don't care what the weather will be.' Newcastle is at his steeliest. 'I need the populace to see that from now on befriending smugglers is a deadly mistake. Nothing will bring them to heel faster, I assure you.'

'Indeed, Thomas.' Henry has finally understood his brother's reasoning. He also understands he is Prime Minister on his brother's say so. Henry has never considered trying to block, or even soften, his brother's draconian Act, the consequence of which has brought them all here this evening. He knows he would not have succeeded, even if he'd tried.

Chapter 49

Tyburn, London
29th July, Dawn

Dawn on a beautiful Monday morning in July. Tyburn is far enough away from the city for the sky to be clear-blue and the air fresh.

William Hogarth pushes his way through the already-growing crowd looking for a good spot to work from. His latest series of twelve engravings is almost complete; he needs another close look at a hanging to make sure the preliminary drawings for the eleventh are accurate. The finished set will tell a tale which warns of the perils of idleness.

He has no idea who will be hanged today (and he doubts any of the condemned men are here through idleness on anyone's part) – but he will make sure that the downfall of his imaginary 'idle prentice' will reflect what he sees happening in front of him. He will make final amendments to his drawing today and send it to the engravers tomorrow; he reckons to have it back by September.

Carpenters are busy putting the final touches to the tree – five men are to hang here today.

The construction is triangular, which allows good views of

death from all sides, and the crossbeams are placed high enough to be seen from a great distance. Most of the expected crowd of thirty thousand at Tyburn are already in or around the site. Those who cannot find space here are already spreading out along the route from Newgate.

Usually on these festival hanging days there will be seventy thousand people along the road. The unusual nature of this particular hanging guarantees the maximum turnout. In total, then, one hundred thousand people intend to have a great day out today, celebrating as five men, none of them known to them, lose their lives. The crush here at the tree itself is expected to be intense – it may even be fatal for some of the revellers if they fall unnoticed underfoot.

Anyone of importance will be sitting in the grandstands finished by the carpenters yesterday. The triangle will have two men hung on each of two sides and just the one man on its third.

It cannot usually be guaranteed that if you have a particular interest in a prisoner he will be brought to the side of the gallows where you sit, but something is different today.

A place has been marked for one particular man to be hung on the side facing Mother Proctor's Pews; he is obviously special.

No one knows who Mother Proctor was, or how she gave this stand its name, but everyone knows it is the best, reserved for ministers, MPs and their guests. Today these VIPs are thought to be very interested in this one death. No-one asks why.

Richard will hang in front of the VIP stand.

What powerful men want, powerful men get.

Chapter 50

Newgate Prison, London
29th July, Dawn

As the same dawn breaks in Newgate, the Ordinary is again in the chapel, holding a final service for the condemned men, the nave dominated by the black coffin. All five members of his congregation are to die today, and he is determined to miss no opportunity to let them do so in a state of grace.

As always on these occasions, most of the congregation show little interest in saving their souls. Taylor can only think that, if they were worried about their souls in the first place, they would not have done the things which have brought them here this morning.

Only Richard pays him attention. His eyes are locked on the Ordinary and he follows the ritual doggedly, as if by doing so he can somehow stop what is to come. He can't of course; apparently not even God can do it.

When the service is finished, they all troop reluctantly down the two flights of stairs which divide the chapel and high hall. There is an anvil in the middle of this hall and here the smiths are waiting to knock off the shackles of the condemned men.

Richard has been here before. He came several days ago and was surrounded by these same men. He had known their trade immediately. He has met many blacksmiths, all good men and true, but these did nothing but lift his arms and look at his legs, their distaste for the state of him clear for anyone to see.

As his leg-irons break he wonders, vaguely, why the smiths had been with him before. No-one had told him, and he hadn't asked.

He thinks, perhaps, he hasn't asked enough questions in his lifetime. He has let others do his thinking for him and it isn't ending well.

Not asking on this occasion, though, was a good decision. The smiths were measuring for the bespoke cage they have made for him at great expense to the state. He will be displayed in it in Shepherd's Bush tonight and stay there until nothing of him remains. Better for him not to know this.

Once his shackles are gone, the warder produces a rope. The noose at one end of it is put over his head, the other ties his hands and is secured round his waist, making it almost as difficult for him to move as the shackles had done.

'Come Richard, time to go.' The Ordinary leads him down to the lodge where the cart is waiting, a coffin there for him to sit on. The mourning bells at St. Sepulchre's, as promised, are already tolling in the background. This time it isn't the crier who intones, but the priests outside the church:

'All good people pray heartily unto God for those poor sinners who are now going to their death, for whom this great bell doth toll.

You that are condemned to die, repent with lamentable tears; ask mercy of the Lord for the salvation of your own souls, through the merits, death, and passion of Jesus Christ, who now

sits at the right hand of God, to make intercession for as many of
you as penitently return unto Him.

Lord have mercy upon you, Christ have mercy upon you.
Lord have mercy upon you, Christ have mercy upon you.

They will repeat this incantation and the bell will toll until the procession is out of sight.

Further opportunity to save the souls of condemned men will come on the next execution day, when the cart comes through the gate carrying a cargo of yet more wretches on their way to Tyburn.

Chapter 51

Newgate, London
29th July, Morning

As the prison gate opens, daylight bursts through, dazzling Richard as he gulps in fresh air. He is astonished to see crowds of people – all driven wild by the sight of the carts coming out of the prison. Showers of vegetables take to the air, landing on the condemned men and their guards at random.

On some carts the prisoners have dressed for the occasion – in wedding suits he supposes – and now stand and wave to the crowd as far as their bonds allow. These are the most hard-boiled villains, not surprised by anything or, apparently, afraid. They have watched this procession many times for other men and are determined to make the best of it. Some have their gallows speeches ready and are rehearsing them to all and sundry as they go.

The crowd pays no attention. The vegetables keep coming. The Ordinary has chosen to travel with Richard on his cart, the last in the procession. By the time they get through the gate everything is at fever pitch.

The Ordinary is reading to him from his bible, but all Richard can think is that it will be hard to spot Jenny in this.

He turns to the Ordinary, the closest thing he has to friend or family now, and shouts above the din. 'Who are all these people?'

How do you tell a man people are rejoicing this much in his impending death? Once again, John Taylor decides to say nothing and returns to reading from his bible in a futile effort to offer comfort in the midst of bedlam.

The Ordinary is ashamed of his fellow men. He knows there will be thousands of people on the road between here and Tyburn, all out to have a festal day while they watch this procession of death. There will be people hanging out of windows, all trying to catch a glimpse of the condemned men. Girls will be blowing kisses, people will be throwing food, others will be cheering or jeering and throwing excrement.

Taylor knows it will take three hours to get to Tyburn, but this, too, he keeps to himself. Whatever the delays, he also knows the condemned men only have a few hours to live – by four o'clock they will all be dead.

The city marshal, the under-marshal and six marshalmen, resplendent in their red uniforms, have picked up and surrounded the procession at the gate. Since 1595 they have been responsible for maintaining order in the city and they're not going to stop now.

No-one must be allowed near any of the carts – last minute escapes and rescues have been tried many times before. By default, the peacekeepers become victims of the vegetable barrage. They are armed, so know they are unlikely to come under serious personal attack – an odd cabbage or carrot can do them no harm.

Richard doesn't know it, because he has never been to London, but he is now traveling along Holborn to St. Giles. All along the route people are venting their feelings on the doomed convicts: cheering some to the echo, offering them nosegays or unlimited drink; railing and storming at those they hate or, worse still, despise.

The Ordinary knows no-one will pay attention to Richard, who sits quietly on the coffin, his eyes fixed permanently on him. Taylor feels that Richard's eyes are asking him questions. Why are we here? Why can't you stop this? Where is your God? Why does he let this happen?

He's wrong, of course. These questions are coming from within himself. Richard has never questioned the existence of God, nor doubted his faithfulness and kindness. Which, in the Ordinary's view, just makes everything worse.

As they go, the crowds get thicker and noisier and Richard finally looks away from the Ordinary and peers outwards, looking for Jenny. He doesn't really think she will be here in this raucous crowd, though. She will be at the end of his journey to help him through his final ordeal, but he keeps looking anyway.

And wonders who is looking after the baby.

Chapter 52

Holborn, London
29th July, Morning

The Mason's Arms stands within a stone's throw of Tyburn and it is here that Richard and his fellow-condemned make the final stop before the last stage of their journey to the tree.

The crowds are particularly thick here. Everyone knows this is the last place for the carts to stop. It happens to allow prisoners to be given food and drink to sustain them for the last few hundred yards. The drink, particularly, is thought by the authorities to be a useful way to keep the prisoners calm in the face of death, the hope being that they will have had enough brandy to fuddle their wits against their fate.

'One for the road!' is the cry. And what a road.

The Ordinary knows Richard has no money, so expects him to remain on the wagon without taking drink. He knows this will mean a lucid death and considers whether he should pay for some brandy for his charge himself.

This turns out not to be necessary.

'Rich! Richard Ashcroft! Come down man.' A voice ringing out from the crowd takes Richard by surprise. Casting about he sees George Crawford offering his hands to help him down off the cart.

'George?' Hope flutters again. The man must be here to save him – he knows more than anyone why none of this should be happening.

'Come down Rich. Come and get brandy. I have it ready for you.' George has been here since dawn, knowing this place will offer his only chance to have contact with his life-long friend who, he well knows, is about to give his life for him.

The city marshal and his men look on. All are particularly on their guard now. Escapes have been made here in the distant past so these days some of the more notorious prisoners have their refreshment manacled to the walls in the cellars; but not even the marshal sees Richard as any kind of threat.

The two men push their way into the inn and George hands Richard the flagon he has waiting for him.

'George – how is this happening to me? You know I am no smuggler – no-one knows it better. Why do they want me to die today?'

George knows only too well why they have chosen Richard for this show. It is aimed at himself, and all the men like him, who have been playing fast and loose with the law for as long as he can remember.

When he first heard what was intended for Richard he was deeply puzzled. Richard, who had so steadfastly refused to have anything to do with smuggling, despite coming under constant pressure to take it up, was the very last person George Crawford had ever expected to see hang. He could think of a hundred or more men who were more likely to be here today.

But over time he has come to see the reasoning behind Newcastle's plan – and he doesn't doubt Newcastle is behind it. There is brilliance in it, and it will serve its purpose well. George does not think he could get Richard to understand

Newcastle's logic if they stayed there for a year. Better just to say something simple.

'They are cruel men, Rich, and you have fallen foul of them in the simplest way. You admitted you helped me and the new law says you must die for it. Not even the King himself could change it.'

'I am dying today because I helped you?'

'In the end, Rich, yes.'

Richard says nothing. It is unfathomable.

George turns to the bar. 'Here, drink this – it will help you on your way. All of it now – there's almost nothing more I can do for you.'

Richard takes the flagon and, obedient to the last, drains it.

'One last thing, Richard. See, here. James is come to be with us.'

Richard is overjoyed. He had not expected this, though he had hoped to catch sight of his wife somewhere. To have James here, close enough to clasp to himself is wonderful beyond imagining.

'James? How did you get here?'

James is a little embarrassed by the embrace, but it has been made clear to him by George; he will never talk to his father again after today. He and Dickon have been at the Nag's Head since before the trial and he knows well what he can and cannot say today.

'I came with Uncle George, father, just as I did for your trial.'

'Where is your mother? Is she here?' He looks around, eagerly searching the crush of people nearby.

James and George have planned for this. The answer is carefully worded. He cannot lie to his father on this of all days.

'No father. She could not come.'

James looks at George pleadingly; he has been told it would

be too cruel to tell his father his mother is dead, even if he does not say how she died. The boy struggles with himself. Surely his father should know? George puts a restraining hand on his shoulder.

'No father. She could not come.'

Chapter 53

Tyburn, London
29th July, Morning

The noise from the not-too-distant crowds tells the gentry in the grandstand that the prisoners are getting close.

'I don't think I can watch this, Henry.' Lady Catherine Manners, wife of Henry Pelham has watched her husband become more and more preoccupied as this day has approached. She knows the witnessing of hangings is a necessary part of his duties, but suspects something about this occasion has been burdening him for some time

After dinner with his brother the previous evening Henry had told all to his wife. She is a gentle soul and cannot forgive Newcastle for engineering this ignominious end for the man Ashcroft; Henry clearly thinks the man should, at worst, be on his way to the colonies.

Not for the first time she wonders whether Henry has paid too high a price to become Prime Minister.

'Catherine, we must.' Pelham is adamant. 'We can show no weakness here – not look away, nothing. If we do, we will send out the message that we have regrets and Thomas will be very angry.'

'But Henry – you do have regrets; I know you do.' Lady Catherine reaches for his hand which he gives.

'That's between you and me Catherine – and will remain so. For now, we must stand together and be strong.'

Indeed they must, for now the sorry procession of carts comes into view. There is a general stirring. High in the grandstand a homing pigeon is released; its arrival back at Newgate will let everyone know that today's grim cargo is safely delivered – none of the condemned men have escaped their fate today. Newcastle gets to his feet, as if to underline the importance of all this to himself.

The first two carts carry two prisoners apiece. No-one knows what their crimes are. It's enough that they are here – they must have done something dreadful to warrant it. One of the men on the leading cart is wearing a white suit and fancy hat. The most hardened criminals always put on a good show for the crowd and this man is doing his bit. The crowd is at fever pitch now and nothing any of the men says has any chance of being heard.

The carts back up to the gallows and the men are brought to their feet. Prisoners' ropes are swung up and over the crossbeams at random with no attempt to adjust the length of drop to their size; their hands are tied behind them. Those first in place must wait for everyone to be ready, and Richard will be the last.

While they're waiting some of the men continue to address the mob and are greeted with fresh onslaughts of vegetables for their trouble.

Richard's cart is backed into position opposite the grandstand so Newcastle and his guests can see clearly what befalls their scapegoat.

The Ordinary is on his feet next to Richard, offering solace, presumably, or at least trying to. Richard stands obediently, quietly, and makes no attempt to address the crowd.

Newcastle is pathetically pleased and relieved about this but quite what he thinks Richard might have achieved by trying to speak to the crowd is not clear. Glad he's not trying to speak, Newcastle is, however, disappointed Ashcroft isn't trying to put up a fight and get away. Isn't, in fact, showing any emotion at all. Everyone seeing the prisoner kicking, screaming and protesting his innocence to the last would better suit his purpose.

The Ordinary continues to speak to Richard for what feels like a very long time. He holds out his hand to comfort him and turns to leave, but almost immediately turns again to answer some query from the condemned man.

That done, he finally leaves.

The five prisoners – four hooded, one not – stand for a short while awaiting their fate. Richard is studying the crowd, searching for someone who will not come.

At a sign from Newcastle the cart drivers slap the hindquarters of the horses, driving them forward and leaving their cargoes dangling from the ropes.

None has the blessing of a broken neck from the drop and all struggle, kick wildly and claw at their throats as suffocation begins to take hold.

Out of the crowd there breaks a fearsome man followed by a younger, leaner youth, heading straight for Richard. George Crawford cuts an imposing, frightening figure and no-one attempts to get in his way.

'Come on James – we must take your father's legs – quickly now to stop his suffering.'

'George. I can't – I can't kill my father.' James was not ready for this and is for a moment rooted to the spot.

'Do it now boy. He's already dying, and no-one else will

save him. If we don't do this, he could suffer here for half an hour or more. All we can do for him now is help him on his way.'

Whether or not James understands this, it is enough to get him moving.

The two of them, man and boy, jump high to grasp the legs which are swinging and jiggling above them. Their full weight is thus brought to bear on the man above, mercifully breaking his neck.

It is impossible to tell whether Richard, unhooded, sees the two of them and knows them as his friend and oldest son; whether he understands enough to know they are doing him an enormous kindness by breaking his neck in this way.

It is entirely possible to know, though, that his last thought is of Jenny.

Newcastle looks on, not happy. He has his death, yes, but not the agonisingly protracted one he would have preferred.

In the end, though, this will have to do.

Chapter 54

Governor of Newgate's House
29th July, Afternoon

On execution days Thomas Banbridge, governor of Newgate, throws banquets which are events not to be missed.

Today the lodge is filled with some thirteen or fourteen people of distinction, and Tilly, his daughter, a very pretty girl, is doing the honours at the table.

Few are doing much justice to the viands: the first call of the inexperienced is for brandy to try and dull the memory.

The only person with a good appetite for Tilly's broiled kidneys, a celebrated dish of hers, is the Ordinary, who has been through this too many times to count and takes it all in his stride.

After breakfast is over the party adjourns to see the cutting down. Carriages are drawn up outside the lodge and now the crowds have thinned the journey which took the carts three hours this morning is over in twenty minutes.

They arrive just as the bodies are being cut down, one by one, ready to be handed to the anatomists. These gentlemen will take the corpses for dissection at the medical school, and everyone agrees this is a fitting end for them.

Some relatives think of rescuing their dead from the fate of dissection and others are desperate to touch the dead men's hands, believing this will give them luck or perhaps a cure. It is always the city marshal and the anatomists who win the fight for the bodies which are taken back to Newgate, still under security, and later to the surgeon's tables. This ensures they will do their fellow men good in death, no matter what harm they did in life.

Today the anatomists will not get their hands on all five corpses. They will not have Richard; he is last to be cut down and, as he falls, the blacksmith's cart comes forward to claim him. The iron cuffs for which he was measured at Newgate are placed round his arms and legs and a chain attached at the back to pull them together, which will make it easy to get him into the cage waiting for him at Shepherd's Bush.

The body posing no further threat, the two smiths take it on, away from Tyburn, west, into the countryside. They travel till dusk and in the last of the fading light they haul the body in its cage up onto the waiting gibbet, there to stay, an example to one and all until it rots away.

Tomorrow the London Gazette will say:

'Yesterday, about eight o'clock Richard Ashcroft was carried under a strong detachment of the guards, from Newgate to Tyburn, and executed pursuant to their sentence; after which his body was hung on a gibbet at Shepherd's Bush, in the Acton Road, near James Hall, who was executed some time since for the murder of his master, Counsellor Penny.'

Indeed. When the sun rose on Shepherd's Bush the morning after his death, Richard's purpose was fully revealed to everyone who passed by. James Hall had been hanging there gibbeted for four years before Richard came to join him.

Richard will be there for a very long time.

Chapter 55

The Ordinary of Newgate's House
29th July, Afternoon

John Taylor is again at his desk. Hanging days are never pleasant but this one was particularly disturbing. He was profoundly touched by the actions of the two men who brought about Richard's death. It seemed to him appropriate that God, in his wisdom, had granted some small solace to Richard Ashcroft, a man who had moved him in ways he preferred not to define.

Life goes on. There's another pamphlet to write and thus it goes:

'Between seven and eight in the morning, Richard Ashcroft went in a cart from Newgate to the place of execution, attended by a company of soldiers, commanded by Lord Manners.

'He behaved with decency, was very attentive, and joined in prayer. When I was about to leave him, after having recommended his soul to Him whose care, Christian charity engages to hope, he will be, Ashcroft begged that the Lord's Prayer might be repeated, to testify his forgiveness of others, as he

hoped for forgiveness, and wished he had been earlier acquainted with that and other parts of devotional service.'

He puts down his pen. Something very wrong happened today. He is a good man but knows his place. There was nothing he could have done to change the outcome, no-one to whom he could appeal. To have done so would anyway have cost him his position. He hopes he did enough to make Richard's final journey a little easier – it was all he could do.

He will pray for Richard and Jenny tonight.

Chapter 56

Newcastle House, London
29th July, Evening

Back in Lincoln's Inn Fields another party is in full swing. The guests here are far more important than those at the Governor of Newgate's banquet. All have been at the hanging.

As Newcastle circulates amongst his guests, he is dismayed to find not everyone has viewed today in the same light as himself.

The snippets of conversation he hears do not please him. Everything cuts through him like a knife. He believes in the process. Others, it now seems, do not.

Really, these people are so ungrateful.

The MP for Maidenhead reaches for more brandy:

'If we take a view of the supposed solemnity from the time at which the criminal leaves the prison to the last moment of his existence, it will be found to be full of the most shocking and disgraceful circumstances.'

. . .

The Lord Chancellor thinks differently:

'*If the only defect were the want of ceremony the minds of the spectators might be left in a state of indifference; but when they view the meanness of the apparatus, the dirty cart and ragged harness, surrounded by a sordid assemblage of the lowest among the vulgar, their sentiments are inclined more to ridicule than pity.*'

Mr Weaving reports:

'*The whole progress is attended by thousands of people. Numbers thicken into a crowd of followers, and an indecent levity is heard.*'

Lord Manners, the city marshal, who had followed the procession from beginning to end:

'*The crowd gathered as it went, the levity increased, till on reaching the fatal tree it became a riotous mob, and their wantonness of speech broke forth in profane jokes, swearing, and blasphemy.*'

The MP for Chichester:

'*The officers of the law were powerless to check the tumult; no attention was paid to the convict's dying speech.*'

The MP for Chichester had not, himself made any attempt to listen either.

Another voice in the melee:

'*Prayers were interrupted, the prisoner's demeanour was*

resigned, and he was sneered at for it. The others were applauded when they went with brazen effrontery to their deaths.'

Does this refer to Richard? Too much!

Newcastle hears all this as he approaches his brother.

'Henry – I do not like what I am hearing here.'

'Why are you surprised Thomas? Your plan required people to be almost as intelligent as you. I feared from the start they would not draw the conclusions from this death you thought they would.'

'When word gets out, they will.' Newcastle's mood is dark, and Henry thinks it's time to go.

Pelham remarks to his wife as they take their leave:

'All the ends of public justice were defeated today; all the effects of example, the terrors of death, the shame of punishment, were all lost in the unseemly celebration of the occasion.'

He's quietly content. He may not have to witness such a sacrifice on his brother's account again.

Catherine thinks her husband is looking rather more cheerful than he has for a while.

Chapter 57

Seaford, Sussex
The Plough Inn

Harvest time, and George Crawford is in the Plough where it all began eighteen years before. He remembers the wedding day of Richard and Jenny, celebrating with them in this place, none of them able to foresee things turning out as they have.

He remembers too well the many occasions in this very bar when he tried to persuade Richard to join him as a lieutenant in his burgeoning gang. Richard, of course, never had inclination to do any such thing.

And yet. And yet it is Richard who has paid the smugglers' ransom, not one of the men gathered here this evening. None of George's gang has yet been caught. He doesn't doubt they will be. Knows many of them will meet the same fate as Richard. Almost certainly it will come to him too.

Many of his men have melted away over the last weeks and he fears the new £500 reward will eventually persuade one of them to give him up. He knows too well that betrayal can come from anywhere these days and £500 will more than make up for the loss of income his men are suffering now the tax cuts have curtailed their operation so drastically.

There will not be much money to be made from smuggling in future and the reward for capture is far higher than before. George is determined to carry on for a short while, but his heart is going out of it. He wanders across to the churchyard and stands under the oak deep in thought. He still sees it as Richard and Jenny's tree even though neither of them will ever come here again.

Richard's corpse is high on display in the Shepherd's Bush.

Blind eyes have been turned again; Jenny's death has been judged an accident and she lies now, with three of her children, at the bottom of the Bishopstone churchyard.

Jenny. He had loved her so, but Richard had won her. At the time he had been glad for her. Richard's goodness would make her far happier than he could ever have done. Now he wonders what would have happened if he had fought harder for her.

Is it his fault, all that has happened? In his own way he has tried always to be a good friend to Richard and has respected his wish not to join his gang. But his friendship has been Richard's undoing. Should he, once he knew the path he was taking, have cut Richard and Jenny off from himself completely, to keep them out of harm's way? He could perhaps have left Richard, but never Jenny.

To have known he must abandon them for their own sakes would have needed him to be able to see far into the future and deep into the mind of Newcastle.

The whole dreadful tale has, after all, come from the mind of Newcastle.

Chapter 58

Bishopstone, Sussex
St Andrew's Churchyard

In the churchyard at Bishopstone James and his younger brother stand at their mother's grave. She would not be here if the minister had not chosen to accept the general view that her fall had been accidental, but the boys do not know this. If they could identify it, their comfort comes from believing neither of their parents ever knew what happened to the other.

Because he was there till the end, James knows Jenny clung to the belief that Richard would be proved innocent and pardoned, though she had no idea how. She knew her husband was a good man who had always done his best to keep the word he had given to her father on their wedding day. 'In sickness and in health, richer and poorer, so long as we both shall live. I promise you James – I meant every word' he had said to his father-in-law, and he had.

Young James had tried so hard to look after his mother in the days after his father was taken. They had all believed Richard would come home one day, but the belief had faded over time until only Jenny hung on. Then, even she had given up. James would never forgive himself for going fishing on the day she died. She had told him to go, but he will always think he should have known what she was doing; that he could have done something which would have kept her with them to this day. He does not believe for one moment her fall was accidental. He wishes he did.

'Mother never doubted Father, Dickon, and nor shall we.'

Dickon, shielded from the worst of the happenings in London, had never doubted him anyway. If he lives long enough to grow to manhood, marry and have children he will name his first son Richard. He is quite resolved on this.

James knows his father never knew his mother had died before him. He hopes he was right to trust George when he said his father should not be told of her death before he died. He also hopes the minister is right, and Jenny was waiting for Richard when he got to heaven – along with Mary Lucy and the twins. His father is happy now if that is so, and he dearly wants him to be happy.

He knows Jenny did not know what fate would befall Richard. She knew he had been taken from her, but he is sure the spectre of the gallows was not one she ever saw. George protected her just enough to stop her from doing so.

For his part, he must look after Dickon.

He does not think he wants to see his godfather again. The grisly scene at Tyburn will always be between them – a memory neither will want to share.

He knows, because his mother said so, that his father's death came directly from his friendship with George, but he doesn't really understand how because he also knows George was there at the end, doing the best he could for Richard right up to the last.

These two things are hard to reconcile.

James's eyes are drawn to the gate in the churchyard wall – the gateway to the land surrounding Bishopstone Place, home of the Duke of Newcastle. It makes him uneasy, and he turns his back on it.

'Come Dickon, we must go on.'

He puts a protective arm round his younger brother's shoulders, and they go on their way – through the lychgate, away from the Duke of Newcastle.

Detail from William Hogarth's preparatory drawing
Plate 11, Industry and Idleness
The Idle 'Prentice Executed at Tyburn
Published September 1747
© Trustees of the British Museum

There were five hanging sessions at Tyburn in 1747. The series 'Industry and Idleness' was published in September of that year and it is entirely possible Hogarth made his drawing two months earlier on the day of Richard's execution.

Interesting to note that there is a blank area at the back of the cart where he later inserted a figure, thought to be John Wesley, as a further support to the moralising nature of the work. One of Hogarth's sponsors and a subscriber to the series was Horace Walpole, son of Sir Robert.

Afterword

'Richard Ashcroft, aged about 44 Years, was born at Lewes in Sussex. From his infancy he was bred to follow the plough, and other parts of husbandry, as his father had done before him, so that his education you may imagine was not much.' The unprompted words of the Ordinary of Newgate; these should frame any view of Richard Ashcroft. This is the man the Ordinary saw.

For those readers not convinced by my narrative that something was very wrong with the way Richard was treated – who think, perhaps, that he was a smuggler after all and my conclusions are not valid – it is worth going back once again to the Ordinary:

'He had a wife and seven children when he was apprehended and brought to Newgate; but since his conviction his wife has died and the seven poor helpless orphans are left without any other provision but what the laws of the land may oblige their native parish to make for their subsistence.'

We have it on very good authority here that Richard was a poor man. No evidence was produced at trial that he had ever been a smuggler and his abject poverty supports his assertion that he never was one.

The amount of money earned by smugglers was enormous. (For those who want to do the maths on the numbers that follow, the value of the pound, according to the Bank of England inflation calculator, has increased 240 times since 1747):

The Parliamentary Committee in 1745 was told the best estimate for how much tea was smuggled annually in England was 3,000,000 lbs. 1,000,000 lbs came in legitimately. Brandy and other spirits were in similar proportions.The retail cost of a pound of tea at the time was anything from 7/6d to 16s, depending on the source. At a conservative average of ten shillings the value of the 3,000,000lbs of tea at that time would be £1,500,000 – 25% of that lost to the revenue in the tea trade alone therefore a represents a huge amount of money.

The smuggling gangs were estimated to be able to bring in 3,000 guineas worth of goods at a time, usually at least once a week. That's £156,000 for each gang annually. There were estimated to be 20,000 smugglers operating in the mid–eighteenth century. Even at fifty men per gang there would be 400 gangs; at £156,000 in tea coffee and spirits each there would be £7,800,000 income between them. In 1747 that represented an enormous amount of money. Smugglers were not poor, not even the lowliest..

Consider also that Richard was tried at the Old Bailey, not in Horsham or East Grinstead which is where a run-of-the mill smuggler from the Sussex coast would have been expected to appear. The Old Bailey was usually reserved for criminals accused of crimes in the City and Middlesex – it wasn't until The Central Criminal Court Act of 1856 that it became normal for people outside those jurisdictions to be tried there. The implication is that the authorities were treating him as a smuggler of some note – at the very least a gang leader or first lieutenant – but nothing in his trial spoke of that. More importantly, such a man would not have been a pauper, which Richard certainly was. It is hard not to conclude that there was some other reason to give him special treatment.

Special treatment, too, in the gibbeting, which was not often used (10% of the very worst murderers) because it was so expensive. Irons and cages had to be specially made-to-measure for each man, at a cost of roughly £50. Why did they think him worthy of this?

By the end of the eighteenth century very little smuggling was taking place. Newcastle's laws were effective and long overdue. Is it really that fanciful to suggest that the use of someone like Richard as an example was exactly what was needed to frighten the populace away from the smugglers who had, up till then, been seen as local heroes?

The outrageousness of the suggestion that a £500 reward should be offered for information leading to the capture of smugglers is hard to put into context in the narrative without breaking the fourth wall. The Bank of England inflation calculator shows this to be the equivalent of £121,287 – a truly life-changing amount.

The names Weaving, Castle and the Widow Kesteven never existed as presented here. Many well known tea, coffee and alcohol merchants have been trading in London from the mid eighteenth century to the present day. Some amassed the wealth which underpins their empires by trading with smugglers, though it is unlikely that any have ever admitted it. Certainly none were ever prosecuted for it.

The smuggler who led the raid on the customs house was hanged at Tyburn six months after Richard. Other events ascribed to George in this book were, in fact, led by similarly ruthless men but are written exactly as described in original sources – always cross-referenced to be sure. George is, therefore, a hybrid smuggler here of my own creation.

Richard's trial transcript and the pamphlets written by the Ordinary are available in the on-line archive of the Old Bailey and have been used verbatim, as indicated in italics in the text. Anything else in italics, such as Pelham's letter, is also quoted verbatim from original text.

All smuggling activity has been drawn from original eye-witness accounts. These are readily available from a host of websites and books on the subject. No incident has been used which does not have multiple sources for verification. An excellent book for anyone wishing to dig deeper into the use of hanging in eighteenth century England, and of smuggling in Sussex (and beyond) in particular, is *Albion's Fatal Tree* by Hay, Limbaugh, Rule, Thompson and Winslow, first published in 1975 and revised in 2011 by Verso.

There is supposition at play in ascribing Jenny's death to suicide. It seems entirely plausible that she would kill herself in the circumstances. Anyone looking at the Ordinary's statement on-line will see that he attributes her death to childbirth. He does not appear to know that by the time of his death Richard had only four of his seven (eight) children left alive, so he is not an entirely reliable source of information about what was happening in Sussex at the time. He may have chosen not to allude to self-murder.

James survived into adulthood and may well have descendants unknown to us.

There is no further record of Ann or Elizabeth after birth. That they survived and were taken into some other family is reasonable speculation.

Dickon Ashcroft survived into old age. He had four children and called the first Richard.

Jenny and the children that died in her lifetime are buried in Bishopstone churchyard. There is no trace that I can find of Ann or Elizabeth anywhere after their birth, both born in Bishopstone.

The Ashcroft family remained in Sussex, in the Seaford area, until 1972. David Ashcroft and his older brother John spent their childhoods messing about in boats in and around Cuckmere Haven and playing on Seaford Head, blissfully unaware of what had happened to their ancestors in those same places. Richard Ashcroft was their seventh great grandfather, Dickon, the sixth. Dickon's son Richard the fifth.

For Book Clubs
Thoughts for discussion...
... and meet the author

Listed below are some discussion points which may be of use to book clubs. Feedback from your meetings would be very welcome.

The author is willing to zoom in to book club meetings at no charge. Please contact her through the contact form on her website www.susanashcroft.co.uk to agree a date.

Any groups such as WIs, history societies, local interest groups or book shops who might like me to come and give a talk about the writing of this book and the wider areas of its subject matter should contact me by the same means.

———

Some general questions you could consider at your meeting
  1 What surprised you most about the book?
  2 Which scene has stuck with you the most?
  3 Did you reread any passages? If so, which ones?
  4 Are there any standout sentences?
  5 Did you race to the end, or was it more of a slow burn?

6 What was your favourite part of the book?

7 What was your least favourite?

9 Did reading the book impact your mood? If yes, how so?

10 Did your opinion of the book change as you read it?

11 If you could ask the author anything, what would it be?

12 Does the book's title work for you?

13 If you could give the book a new title, what would it be?

14 Will you remember it in a few months or years?

15 Are there things you're still thinking about?

16 Would you ever consider re-reading it?

17 Did the book strike you as original?

18 Is this book rooted in its time, or timeless?

Questions relating to characters

1 Describe the relationship between Richard and Jenny

2 Describe the relationship between Richard and George

3 George is both good and bad. Which is more important?

4 Does the behaviour of Newcastle feel contemporary?

5 Are you persuaded that Richard is treated badly?

Questions directly from the author:

1 Did you know what happened before you read the book?

2 If you did, how did that influence the way you read it?

3 If you did not, describe what you felt as it played out.

4 Which shelf in the bookshop should this book sit on?

5 I chose to write this in the present tense. Why?

Acknowledgements

I would not have written this had I not come upon the comprehensive on-line resource at https://www. oldbaileyonline.org (*June 1747, trial of Richard Ashcroft* (t17470604-13). To be able to read first-hand the words of John Taylor the Ordinary and to read the trial transcript was extraordinary; scans of the original documentation made it even more so.

Slowly but surely I started to discover a world I knew nothing about, even though I had grown up in Sussex right where some of the worst smuggling gangs operated. Initial contact with https://leweshistory.org.uk pointed me towards records at https://www.thekeep.info where I was able to find Richard, Jenny and the children in records from long ago, and detailed information about the Duke of Northumberland.

Smuggling incidents in the book all happened as written, though names and dates have been changed to allow me leeway on where I could use them. The unfortunate Challis and Barrow were in fact Daniel Chater and William Galley, whose story can be found on line in numerous places, including www. nationalarchives.org.uk.

An excellent book for in-depth background information about crime and society in eighteenth-century England, with a great section on smuggling is *Albion's Fatal Tree* by Hay, Linebaugh, Rule, Thompson and Winslow, first published in 1975 and updated in 2011 by Verso.

A very useful website was www.smuggling.co.uk from which I was able to jump off into further research as I fell deeper and deeper down the smuggling rabbit hole towards the Hawkhurst Gang - perhaps the most notorious of the smuggling gangs which operated mainly in Kent. Much of what I have attributed to George Crawford's gang was in fact done by the Hawkhurst thugs.

We were lucky to come across Arwen Folkes, vicar of St Andrews, Bishopstone who pointed out the places in her beautiful church that would have been seen by Richard and Jenny, including the font where most of their children must have been baptised. Sadly we could not identify the spot where Jenny and at least two of her children are buried, but it was enough to know that we were close.

My friend Gay Scott was the first to see the initial synopsis and preface. My thanks go to her for being exceptionally supportive in those tentative early days. The ladies of our book circle, and my sister Nina, were the first to see the initial 'finished' draft and I am profoundly grateful for the encouragement they gave me to see the project through. They identified a number of areas that needed expansion or clarification and were absolutely right in every case.

Thinking the book complete I sent it to Paul Jesson, whose opinion I value highly. He read it, loved it, then proceeded to demonstrate that it really wasn't complete after all. He threw himself into checking every detail, researching all aspects and feeding back suggestions, almost all of which I happily adopted. He was, in fact, my editor, and finally put the icing on the cake by drawing the map which is now handily placed at the front of the book to keep everyone orientated. Not content with that, he followed it up with the lovely little line drawings which are dotted through the book.

Paul approached his designer friend Clare Nicholson and

together they developed the cover with amazing speed and accuracy. The atmospheric photograph of the Cuckmere winding its way to the Haven was exactly the right choice; this book is historical but also contemporary, dealing as it does with corruption in high places. The timelessness of the shot is what drew me to it - I doubt the view has changed in the intervening 275 years since Richard fished there.

Finally my thanks must go to my husband, David. As I say in the dedication, it was his wish for an ancestor of note that brought me here. His enthusiasm and support throughout the whole project has been invaluable. I hope he is now suitably ancestored up!

About the Author

Susan Ashcroft was born in Brighton and grew up in West Sussex. After studying music at the Guildhall School of Music and Drama she taught at The Mount School in York before moving to London where she met her husband David.

For twenty-five years Susan and David, together with their three children, Thom, Sophie and Ben, lived in Northern Ireland where for seven years she was the Marketing Manager of the Ulster Orchestra.

On retirement she moved to Norfolk and began researching family history which is where she came upon the extraordinary story of David's ancestor Richard Ashcroft, who, in 1747, became the first man hanged for being associated with smugglers under the terms of a new Act of Parliament which was passed in 1746.

Never having written anything before, Susan found herself so immersed in Richard's story she felt she had to put pen to paper and bring it to a wider audience.

She harbours a secret desire to one day see Richard Ashcroft cleared of what she believes were politically expedient trumped-up charges which should never have been brought against him.

Printed in Great Britain
by Amazon

78152765R00147